Classic Horse Stories

Classic Horse Stories

COMPILED BY CHRISTINA ROSSETTI DARLING

AND BLUE LANTERN STUDIO

chronicle books · san francisco

Library of Congress Cataloging-in-Publication Data available.
ISBN 978-0-8118-6569-2

Book design by Stephanie Bart-Horvath.
Typeset in Cg Cloister.

Manufactured by C & C Offset, Longgang, Shenzhen, China, in June 2010.

1 3 5 7 9 10 8 6 4 2

This product conforms to CPSIA 2008.

Chronicle Books LLC
680 Second Street
San Francisco, California 94107

www.chroniclekids.com

For my wonderful mother, who helps me so much in every way imaginable,
and Jason and Lilly, who are the flame around which I flutter.

Many thanks to Shane Flores, for research help and encouragement,
Lia Friedman, Benjamin Darling, and my father, Harold Darling.

Contents

B.BUTLER

Foal

BY MARY BRITTON MILLER

Come trotting up
Beside your mother,
Little skinny.
Lay your neck across
Her back, and whinny,
Little foal.
You think you're a horse
Because you can trot,
But you're not.
Your eyes are so wild,
And each leg is as tall
As a pole;
And you're only a skittish
Child, after all,
Little foal.

Black Beauty

(An excerpt from "My Early Home" chapter)

BY ANNA SEWELL

THE FIRST PLACE THAT I can well remember was a large pleasant meadow with a pond of clear water in it. Some shady trees leaned over it, and rushes and water lilies grew at the deep end. Over the hedge on one side we looked into a plowed field, and on the other we looked over a gate at our master's house, which stood by the roadside; at the top of the meadow was a grove of fir trees, and at the bottom a running brook overhung by a steep bank.

While I was young, I lived upon my mother's milk, as I could not eat grass. In the daytime I ran by her side, and at night I lay down close by her. When it was hot we used to stand by the pond in the shade of the trees, and when it was cold we had a nice warm shed near the grove.

As soon as I was old enough to eat grass, my mother used to go out to work in the daytime and come back in the evening.

There were six young colts in the meadow besides me; they were older than I was; some were nearly as large as grown-up horses. I used to run with them and had great fun; we used to gallop all together round and round the field as hard as we could go. Sometimes we had rather rough play, for they would frequently bite and kick as well as gallop.

One day, when there was a good deal of kicking, my mother whinnied to me to come to her, and then she said:

"I wish you to pay attention to what I am going to say to you. The colts who live here are very good colts, but they are cart-horse colts, and of course they have not learned manners. You have been well-bred and well-born; your father has a great name in these parts, and your grandfather won the cup two years at the Newmarket races; your grandmother had the sweetest temper of any horse I ever knew, and I think you have never seen me kick or bite. I hope you will grow up gentle and good, and never learn bad ways; do your work with a good will, lift your feet up well when you trot, and never bite or kick even in play."

I have never forgotten my mother's advice; I knew she was a wise old horse, and our master thought a great deal of her. Her name was Duchess, but he often called her Pet.

Our master was a good, kind man. He gave us good food, good lodging, and kind words; he spoke as kindly to us as he did to his little children. We were all fond of him, and my mother loved him very much. When she saw him at the gate, she would neigh with joy and trot up to him. He would pat and stroke her and say, "Well, old Pet, and how is your little Darkie?" I was a dull black, so he called me Darkie; then he would give me a piece of bread, which was very good, and sometimes he brought a carrot for my mother. All the horses would come to him, but I think we were his favorites. My mother always took him to the town on a market day in a light gig.

FREE
STRAWBERRY
ROAN
RODEO
STATE FAIR
SEPT. 26
TO
OCT. 1

The Story of the First Woman Bucking Bronc Rider

BY MILT RISKE

A HUSH SETTLED OVER the crowd at Cheyenne Frontier Days, in 1904, when it was announced that Bertha Kalpernik was going to ride the bucking horse Tombstone. Even range-hardened men used to the women helping with ranch chores had their doubts. The horse was led to the front of the grandstand. One of the mounted arena attendants held the horse securely by lariat. Another cowboy placed a blindfold—a gunnysack or a canvas strip—across the horse's eyes, and another attempted to saddle the usually less than docile animal. Once the horse was saddled, the young cowgirl climbed aboard and, at her nod, the snubber released the snorting brute. A good snubber holding the horse was the prerequisite to a good ride.

Bertha made a good ride—how long it was is not recorded. In early rodeo, there was no eight-second rule; when the judge figured the beast had been bested by the rider, the contest was over. Some rides may have lasted as long as 20 seconds to two minutes. The first lady bronc rider in Cheyenne won the plaudits of the crowd, and a Cheyenne newspaper reported that the throng "had many misgivings" in seeing a young cowgirl aboard a pitching horse. The account continued, "The victory was won and the horse had been broken."

The Cowgirl

(An excerpt)

BY E. A. BRININSTOOL

She ain't inclined to'rds lots o'things
That Eastern gals can do up brown;
She don't wear jewelry and rings,
Like them swell girls what lives in town.
Her cheeks are tanned an olive tint,
That shows the roses hidin' there;
Her eyes are brown, and there's a hint
Of midnight in her wavin' hair.

She don't go in for fancy hats;
A wide-brimmed Stetson is her pet;
She has no use for puffs and rats;
A harem skirt would make her fret.
She wears a kerchief 'round her neck
At breaking broncs she shows her sand,
And at a roundup she's on deck,
And twirls a rope with a practiced hand.

She doesn't know a thing about
Them motor cars that buzz and whirr,
But when she goes a-ridin' out,
A tough cow-pony pleases her.
Her hands are tanned to match her cheeks;
Her smile will start your heart a-whirl,
And when she looks at you and speaks,
You love this rosy, wild cowgirl!

The Red Pony

(An excerpt)

BY JOHN STEINBECK

JODY'S FATHER UNHOOKED THE door and they went in. They had been walking toward the sun on the way down. The barn was black as night in contrast and warm from the hay and from the beasts. Jody's father moved over toward the one box stall. "Come here!" he ordered. Jody could begin to see things now. He looked into the box stall and then stepped back quickly.

A red pony colt was looking at him out of the stall. Its tense ears were forward and a light of disobedience was in its eyes. Its coat was rough and thick as an Airedale's fur and its mane was long and tangled. Jody's throat collapsed in on itself and cut his breath short.

"He needs a good currying," his father said, "and if I ever hear of you not feeding him or leaving his stall dirty, I'll sell him off in a minute."

Jody couldn't bear to look at the pony's eyes any more. He gazed down at his hands for a moment, and he asked very shyly, "Mine?" No one answered him. He put his hand out toward the pony. Its gray nose came close, sniffing loudly, and then the lips drew back and the strong teeth closed on Jody's fingers. The pony shook its head up and down and seemed to laugh with amusement. Jody regarded his bruised fingers. "Well," he said with pride—"Well, I guess he can bite all right." The two men laughed, somewhat in relief. Carl Tiflin went out of the barn and walked up a side-hill to be by himself, for he was embarrassed, but Billy Buck stayed. It was easier to talk to Billy Buck. Jody asked again—"Mine?"

Billy became professional in tone. "Sure! That is, if you look out for him and break him right. I'll show you how. He's just a colt. You can't ride him for some time."

Jody put out his bruised hand again, and this time the red pony let his nose be rubbed. "I ought to have a carrot," Jody said. "Where'd we get him, Billy?"

"Bought him at a sheriff's auction," Billy explained. "A show went broke in Salinas and had debts. The sheriff was selling off their stuff."

The pony stretched out his nose and shook the forelock from his wild eyes. Jody stroked the nose a little. He said softly, "There isn't a saddle?"

Billy Buck laughed. "I'd forgot. Come along."

In the harness room, he lifted down a little saddle of red morocco leather. "It's just a show saddle," Billy Buck said disparagingly. "It isn't practical for the brush, but it was cheap at the sale."

Jody couldn't trust himself to look at the saddle either, and he couldn't speak at all. He brushed the shining red leather with his fingertips, and after a long time he said, "It'll look pretty on him though." He thought of the grandest and prettiest things he knew. "If he hasn't a name already, I think I'll call him Gabilan Mountains," he said.

Billy Buck knew how he felt. "It's a pretty long name. Why don't you just call him Gabilan? That means hawk. That would be a fine name for him." Billy felt glad. "If you will collect tail hair, I might be able to make a hair rope for you sometime. You could use it for a hackamore."

Jody wanted to go back to the box stall. "Could I lead him to school, do you think—to show the kids?"

But Billy shook his head. "He's not even halter broke yet. We had a time getting him here. Had to almost drag him. You better be starting for school though."

"I'll bring the kids to see him here this afternoon," Jody said.

Six boys came over the hill half an hour early that afternoon, running hard, their heads down, their forearms working, their breath whistling. They swept by the house and cut across the stubble-field to the barn. And then they stood self-consciously before the pony, and then they looked at Jody with eyes in which there was a new admiration and a new respect. Before today Jody had been a boy, dressed in overalls and a blue shirt—quieter than most, even suspected of being a little cowardly. And now he was different. Out of a thousand centuries, they drew the ancient admiration of the footman for the horseman. They knew instinctively that a man on a horse is spiritually as well as physically bigger than a man on foot. They knew that Jody had been miraculously lifted out of equality with them, and had been placed over them. Gabilan put his head out of the stall and sniffed them.

"Why'n't you ride him?" the boys cried. "Why'n't you braid his tail with ribbons like in the fair?" "When you going to ride him?"

Jody's courage was up. He too felt the superiority of the horseman. "He's not old enough. Nobody can ride him for a long time. I'm going to train him on the long halter. Billy Buck is going to show me how."

"Well, can't we even lead him around a little?"

"He isn't even halter-broke," Jody said. He wanted to be completely alone when he took the pony out for the first time. "Come and see the saddle."

They were speechless at the red morocco saddle, completely shocked out of comment. "It isn't much use in the brush," Jody explained. "It'll look pretty on him though. Maybe I'll ride bareback when I go into the brush."

"How you going to rope a cow without a saddle horn?"

"Maybe I'll get another saddle for every day. My father might want me to help him with the stock." He let them feel the red saddle and showed them the brass chain throat-latch on the bridle and the big brass buttons at each temple where the headstall and brow band crossed. The whole thing was too wonderful. They had to go away after a little while, and each boy, in his mind, searched among his possessions for a bribe worthy of offering in return for a ride on the red pony when the time should come.

Jody was glad when they had gone. He took brush and currycomb from the wall, took down the barrier of the box stall, and stepped cautiously in. The pony's eyes glittered, and he edged around into kicking position. But Jody touched him on the shoulder and rubbed his high arched neck as he'd always seen Billy Buck do, and he crooned, "So-o-o, boy," in a deep voice. The pony gradually relaxed his tenseness. Jody curried and brushed until a pile of dead hair lay in the stall and until the pony's coat had taken on a deep red shine. Each time he finished he thought it might have been done better. He braided the mane into a dozen little pigtails, and he braided the forelock, and then he undid them and brushed the hair out straight again.

Jody did not hear his mother enter the barn. She was angry when she came, but when she looked in at the pony and at Jody working over him, she felt a curious pride rise up in her. "Have you forgot the wood-box?" she asked gently. "It's not far off from dark and there's not a stick of wood in the house, and the chickens aren't fed."

Jody quickly put up his tools. "I forgot, ma'am."

"Well, after this do your chores first then you won't forget. I expect you'll forget lots of things now if I don't keep an eye on you."

"Can I have carrots from the garden for him, ma'am?"

She had to think about that. "Oh—I guess so, if you only take the big tough ones."

"Carrots keep the coat good," he said, and again she felt the curious rush of pride.

Jody never waited for the triangle to get him out of bed after the coming of the pony. It became his habit to creep out of bed even before his mother was awake, to slip into his clothes, and to go quietly down to the barn to see Gabilan. In the gray quiet mornings, when the land and the brush and the houses and the trees were silver-gray and black like a photograph negative, he stole toward the barn, past the sleeping stones and the sleeping cypress tree. The turkeys, roosting in the tree out of coyotes' reach, clicked drowsily. The fields glowed with a gray frostlike light, and in the dew the tracks of rabbits and of field mice stood out sharply. The good dogs came stiffly out of their little houses, hackles up and deep growls in their throats. Then they caught Jody's scent, and their stiff tails rose up and waved a greeting—Doubletree Mutt with the big thick tail, and Smasher, the incipient shepherd—then went lazily back to their warm beds.

It was a strange time and a mysterious journey, to Jody—an extension of a dream. When he first had the pony, he liked to torture himself during the trip by thinking Gabilan would not be in his stall and, worse, would never have been there. And he had other delicious little self-induced pains. He thought how the rats had gnawed ragged holes in the red saddle, and how the mice had nibbled Gabilan's tail until it was stringy and thin. He usually ran the last little way to the barn. He unlatched the rusty hasp of the barn door and stepped in, and no matter how quietly he opened the door, Gabilan was always looking at him over the barrier of the box stall and Gabilan whinnied softly and stamped his front foot, and his eyes had big sparks of red fire in them like oakwood embers.

Sometimes, if the workhorses were to be used that day, Jody found Billy Buck in the barn harnessing and currying. Billy stood with him and looked long at Gabilan and he told Jody a great many things about horses. He explained that they were terribly afraid for their feet, so that one must make a practice of lifting the legs and patting the hoofs and ankles to remove their terror. He told Jody how horses love conversation. He must talk to the pony all the time, and tell him the reasons for everything. Billy wasn't sure a horse could understand everything that was said to him, but it was impossible to say how much was understood. A horse never kicked up a fuss if someone he liked explained things to him. Billy could give examples, too. He had known, for instance, a horse nearly dead beat with fatigue to perk up when told it was only a little farther to his destination. And he had known a horse paralyzed with fright to come out of it when his rider told him what it was that was frightening him. While he talked in the mornings, Billy Buck cut twenty or thirty straws into neat three-inch lengths and stuck them into his hatband. Then, during the whole day, if he wanted to pick his teeth or merely to chew on something, he had only to reach up for one of them.

Jody listened carefully, for he knew, and the whole county knew, that Billy Buck was a fine hand with horses. Billy's own horse was a stringy cayuse with a hammer head, but he nearly always won first prize at the stock trials. Billy could rope a steer, take a double half-hitch about the horn with his riata, and dismount, and his horse would play the steer as an angler plays a fish, keeping a tight rope until the steer was down or beaten.

Every morning, after Jody had curried and brushed the pony, he let down the barrier of the stall, and Gabilan thrust past him and raced down the barn and into the corral. Around and around he galloped, and sometimes he jumped forward and landed on stiff legs. He stood quivering, stiff ears forward, eyes rolling so that the whites showed, pretending to be frightened. At last he walked snorting to the water-trough and buried his nose in the water up to the nostrils. Jody was proud then, for he knew that was the way to judge a horse. Poor horses only touched their lips to the water, but a fine spirited beast put his whole nose and mouth under, and only left room to breathe.

Then Jody stood and watched the pony, and he saw things he had never noticed about any other horse, the sleek, sliding flank muscles and the cords of the buttocks, which flexed like a closing fist, and the shine the sun put on the red coat. Having seen horses all his life, Jody had never looked at them very closely before. But now he noticed the moving ears, which gave expression and even inflection of expression to the face. The pony talked with his ears. You could tell exactly how he felt about everything by the way his ears pointed. Sometimes they were stiff and upright and sometimes lax and sagging. They went back when he was angry or fearful, and forward when he was anxious and curious and pleased; and their exact position indicated which emotion he had.

Billy Buck kept his word. In the early fall the training began. First there was the halter-breaking, and that was the hardest because it was the first thing. Jody held a carrot and coaxed and promised and pulled on the rope. The pony set his feet like a burro when he felt the strain. But before long he learned. Jody walked all over the ranch leading him. Gradually, he took to dropping the rope until the pony followed him unled wherever he went.

And then came the training on the long halter. That was slower work. Jody stood in the middle of a circle, holding the long halter. He clucked with his tongue and the pony started to walk in a big circle, held in by the long rope. He clucked again to make the pony trot and again to make him gallop. Around and around Gabilan went thundering and enjoying it immensely. Then he called, "Whoa," and the pony stopped. It was not long until Gabilan was perfect at it. But in many ways he was a bad pony. He bit Jody in the pants and stomped on Jody's feet. Now and then his ears went back and he aimed a tremendous kick at the boy. Every time he did one of these bad things, Gabilan settled back and seemed to laugh to himself.

The Old Brown Horse

BY J. YORKE BAILEY

The old brown horse looks over the fence
In a weary sort of way;
He seems to be saying to all who pass:
"Well, folks, I've had my day—
I'm simply watching the world go by,
And nobody seems to mind
As they're dashing past in their motorcars,
A horse who is lame and half blind."

The old brown horse has a shaggy coat,
But once he was young and trim,
And he used to trot through the woods and lanes
With the man who was fond of him.
But his master rides in a motorcar,
And it makes him feel quite sad
When he thinks of the days that used to be,
And of all the times they had.

Sometimes a friendly soul will stop
Near the fence, where the tired old head
Rests wearily on the topmost bar,
And a friendly word is said.
Then the old brown horse gives a little sigh
As he feels the kindly touch
Of a hand on his mane or his shaggy coat,
And he doesn't mind so much.

So if you pass by the field one day,
Just stop for a word or two
With the old brown horse who was once as young
And as full of life as you.
He'll love the touch of your soft young hand,
And I know he'll seem to say—
"Oh, thank you, friend, for the kindly thought
For a horse who has had his day."

The Horse

BY WILLIAM SHAKESPEARE

I will not change my horse with any that treads. . . .
When I bestride him, I soar, I am a hawk.
He trots the air; the earth sings when he touches it.
The basest horn of his hoof is more musical
Than the pipe of Hermes.
He's of the color of the nutmeg and of the heat of the ginger. . . .
He is pure air and fire, and the dull elements
Of earth and water never appear in him,
But only in patient stillness while his rider mounts him. . . .
It is the prince of palfreys: his neigh is like
The bidding of a monarch, and his countenance
Enforces homage.

The Plug-Horse Derby

(An excerpt from "The Secret Word" chapter)

BY EMMA L. BROCK

AT LAST IT WAS half past twelve.

"Well, guess we'd better start," said Nancy's father. "It is a good walk over to the grandstand."

"He said one o'clock sharp," said Nancy. Nancy was brushing Plow Boy's neck and sides and back. She brushed at his mane and tail. She ran her fingers over the long black hairs of his mane. That was one of his beauties, she thought. He seemed to like it, too. He always seemed to like to toss it so that it flopped on his neck, and it fluttered beautifully when he was running.

"OK, Nance?" her father asked.

"Oh, sure," Nancy said. Her father helped her mount Plow Boy. Then she and Bill on their horses strolled over toward the grandstand.

There were several horses coming along the roadways from different directions. Nancy saw the redheaded boy leading his roan horse. His hair certainly was red. It looked redder than ever in the noon sun.

At the grandstand, the stewards who had helped with the weighing were now sorting the horses. They were putting the horses together in groups, those of similar size in a group.

"Nancy Jane Reed," one of them was calling.

"Nancy Jane Reed, 1540 pounds." Nancy's father snorted with laughter.

"Nancy Jane Reed, 1540 pounds," he repeated. He was laughing so hard that her mother led him away to their seats in the grandstand, where they were to watch the races.

"William McIntire, 1500 pounds."

"Olaf Olson, 1495 pounds. You three will be the fifth race," the man said. "Wait over there in the shade of the grandstand until we call you. Race number five, remember."

From behind the grandstand, Nancy could not see anything that went on. She could hear the men's voices calling and directing. Other horses and jockeys came into the shade near them. The two boys in the fifth race were looking Plow Boy over.

"He sure is a big horse," one of the boys said, the one called William.

"But big horses can't run so fast," said the other boy.

"He can run all right," Nancy told them.

"Girls can't ride anyway," William said. "They aren't strong enough."

"You haven't a chance," said Olaf.

"Too bad." Nancy patted Plow Boy's neck and ran her fingers down his mane. She grinned to herself. The boys did not know about the secret word.

"And we won't tell, P. B., will we? That secret word!"

"Are you the only girl in the races?" Olaf asked.

"No, there's another one over there and there's another."

"Girls can't ride."

"Haw," the boys taunted. "Girls can't ride! You show me."

"OK, I will," Nancy said. "You wait and see. You may get a surprise." Nancy could see Bill far down the line. Pete was dancing. She wondered what race Bill was in. Two men came along to see that everything was all right and that all the horses were behaving and the jockeys, too. "Twon't be long now," one of them said. "We start in just a minute. Remember your race number."

Then they could hear the shout over the loudspeaker. "Race number one. Contestants will bring their horses around to the track. Race number one!"

The voice sent shivers down Nancy's spine and out into her fingers and toes. It was the beginning. She wished she were in the first race.

"P. B.," she said in his ear.

Plow Boy nickered a gentle little nicker. It sounded like: "Don't worry, old girl, we'll do it." There was the sound of shouting voices and orders, then the thudding of horses' hoofs. In less than a minute it was over. There was shouting and clapping for the winner.

"Race number two!" the megaphone thundered. It was coming nearer, Nancy thought. She fiddled with Plow Boy's bridle. She turned around and straightened his tail. She leaned over and looked at his left foot. Why his left foot, she did not know. It had not been bothering him. It was just to be busy.

"Race number three!" called the megaphone.

"Oh," Nancy groaned to herself.

The two boys who were racing against her were studying Plow Boy again. "Too bad he's so big and clumsy," William said. Nancy smiled so they would not know how scared she was.

"Too bad you're a girl, too," the other boy said.

"You're too little for that horse. You'll never manage him. Ole here is just the right size." He slapped his white horse's neck. "Good old Ole!" he said.

"You're awful little," said William.

"How old are you?" asked Olaf.

"Eleven—going on twelve," Nancy answered.

"Huh! You're just a baby. We're fourteen."

Nancy smiled harder so that they would not know that she was a little cross. That was Bill's age, too, and they were just like Bill. She guessed boys were all alike. Oafs. Just oafs!

"Race number four!" bellowed the megaphone. Nancy could not see Bill anywhere. Had he been in one of the races already finished?

"Come on, now," one of the men said. "Get ready. You're next, number five. Move up to the gate to be ready."

The three horses stepped out of the shade into the hot sunlight and along the road to the gate of the racetrack. The fourth racehorses were pounding their quarter-mile to victory. There were hundreds of people in the grandstand. They were shouting and urging the riders on. Then the race was over and the horses loped on around the track.

"Head up, P. B.," Nancy ordered. "Remember the secret word."

"Race number five!" the megaphone shouted.

At the word *five*, the tingles began galloping up and down Nancy as fast as she meant to race Plow Boy. Nancy and the two boys rode up the bank to the track and around to the starting place.

"There you are," said one of the men.

"Steady!"

"Nance, Nance." It was Johnny calling. "Steve's at the finish line waiting for you."

Nancy was too excited to answer. The man in charge was saying: "When the flag drops, watch the flag. Now, steady, steady. Hold that horse there. Go!" and down went the flag. The horses took off!

Nancy crouched over Plow Boy's neck as he leaped into the lead. He had a good head start, but Nancy could see the white horse creeping up beside her, that white horse Ole.

"Come on, Ole. Come on, Ole!" the boy was shouting. He was hitting at him with a little whip. Ole darted forward. He was ahead of Plow Boy.

Nancy leaned over and spoke the secret word in Plow Boy's ear. "Oats, P. B.! Oats, oats!" Plow Boy lifted his head. "Oats!" shouted Nancy.

Plow Boy did not see any oats, but he trusted Nancy. He gathered his feet under him and, at the turn of the track, he plunged ahead of the white horse.

"Oats!" shouted Nancy, and Plow Boy doubled his feet up faster and thundered his way over the finish line.

"Ahead by a length!" shouted the official as he swung down the flag. "The big black ahead by a length."

Nancy leaned back and pulled on Plow Boy's reins. "OK," she whispered. "Good boy, good boy, P. B. You did it. You did it. I knew you would."

Plow Boy was blowing big breaths through his nostrils. He whinnied.

"Yes, P. B., we'll go get the oats right now. Dad has the feedbag, and he'll meet us at the gate. Good boy!"

"Hi, Nance," yelled Steve, waving his camera. "I got you, Nance. I got you. We're proud of you!"

"Thanks, Steve," squeaked Nancy. Her voice seemed to be stuck. The megaphone was calling for the sixth race. And there was Johnny waving his notebook and shouting.

"Good for you, Nance. Nancy Jane Reed, the fabulous jockey. It's all down here, Nance. In the paper tomorrow."

"Thanks, Johnny," Nancy said. Her voice was coming back again. Would Johnny ask her for her autograph? But he did not. Nancy led the way back. She had won the race!

William and Olaf did not have a word to say about too-big horses and too-little girls. They just quietly followed Nancy and Plow Boy from the track.

It was a hot ride back home after Plow Boy had finished his oats and hay and Nancy had devoured two double ice cream cones. They were both glad to reach home. Plow Boy was rubbed down and so was Pete when he and Bill straggled in. Then the family sat down to supper. It was good, and the whole family, including Jens, ate quantities of food. Nancy was very quiet during supper, even though she was nearly bursting with happiness. She was quiet because Bill had not won his race. She just ate her supper and did not say a word.

"What happened, Bill? Tell us what happened," his father said, and for once he was not laughing.

"It was Pete," Bill said. "Something got into him."

"What did he do, Bill?" Jens asked. "He's really a good horse."

"And what made him do it?" asked Bill's mother.

"He was contrary all morning. Remember I told you?"

"Yes," his father said.

"He was going all right until we came to the turn. He was running good till we came to the turn!"

"Then what, Bill?"

"And then what did the idiot do?" cried Bill in disgust. "Did he go round the turn like any sane horse? No! No! He went around the turn and then kept right on turning. He ran in a half-circle and jumped over the fence into the center where the grass is. And then he did the other half of the circle and jumped the fence onto the track again and ran the other way. It almost jarred my teeth out. That crazy horse!"

"Bad luck, Bill," said his father.

"Too bad," his mother said.

"He needs a bigger track," said Jens.

"He's an idiot horse," said Bill, grinding his teeth.

"He was excited, maybe," Nancy said. "He wanted to win the race so much that he got mixed up. Sorry, Bill."

"Yes, and that plug horse of yours, he never gets excited. That's a good name for him, Plow Boy. He's just a stodgy plow horse. He just runs and runs. He's too stupid to do anything else."

"Bill!" gasped Nancy.

"Plow Boy is a good horse, Bill," his father said.

"He's a good horse and he's fast. He deserved to win. And Nance is a good rider."

"Tell you what, Bill," said his father. "That Pete is a good jumping horse. We'll have to enter him in the next hurdle race we hear about."

"He could jump the tallest hedge in England," said Jens. "I'll bet he could."

"And I'll bet he could, too," said Bill's father, with his rumbling laugh. "He's a hurdle horse, not just a quarter-mile racer. He was in the wrong race, Bill."

"Steeplechase for him!" Bill began to laugh. "Sure!" And he laughed so hard that he nearly choked on his salad. To think of that dumb horse taking the trouble to jump hurdles when all he needed to do was some fast galloping.

"Train him for the steeplechase, Bill," said Jens.

"Don't know that he needs any more training, Bill," his father said. "He's ready now."

They all laughed, even Bill's mother, all except Nancy. She could hardly keep her laughter in. Her shoulders shook with it. But she thought she really should not laugh out loud when her horse had won and Bill's horse had only jumped fences.

The Legend of Pegasus

BY E. AND J. LEHNER

THE WHITE, WINGED HORSE of ancient legend, Pegasus, was the most gentle of all fabled creatures.

According to Greek mythology, it was believed to have been created by Poseidon from the bloody head of the slain Gorgon Medusa.

Caught and tamed by Athena, it became the steed of the Corinthian folk hero Bellerophon in his fight with the monster Chimera and in his other adventures.

When Bellerophon, riding Pegasus, tried to reach the dwelling of the gods on Mount Olympus, he was thrown by the flying horse; Pegasus reached the summit alone and became the Thundering Horse of Jove, carrier of the divine lightning bolts. He was placed as a permanent constellation among the stars.

In pre-classical times, the figure of the sky-horse was used in astrology by the Assyrian-Babylonians, the Etruscans, the Hittites, and the early Aryans.

Its name derives from the Phoenician *pag sus*, the "bridled horse." In later tradition, Pegasus became the symbolic mount of poets and artists because of Greek legend, which said that with a stamp of his hoof, he caused the flow of Hippocrene, the fountain of the Muses, on Mount Helicon. Thus, Pegasus became the symbol of poetic inspiration and the emblem of creative arts.

Pegasus

BY ELEANOR FARJEON

From the blood of Medusa
Pegasus sprang.
His hoof of heaven
Like melody rang.
His whinny was sweeter
Than Orpheus' lyre.
The wing on his shoulder
Was brighter than fire.
His tail was a fountain,
His nostrils were caves,
His mane and his forelock
Were musical waves.
He neighed like a trumpet,
He cooed like a dove,
He was stronger than terror
And swifter than love.
He could not be captured,
He could not be bought,
His rhythm was running,
His standing was thought.
With one eye on sorrow
And one eye on mirth,
He galloped in heaven
And gamboled on earth.
And only the poet
With wings to his brain
Can mount him and ride him
Without any rein.
The stallion of heaven,
The steed of the skies,
The horse of the singer
Who sings as he flies.

Five O'Clock Charlie

BY MARGUERITE HENRY

CHARLIE WAS A BIG old workhorse with sad brown eyes and shaggy feathers on his feet. He belonged to Mister Spinks, a lean, weathered man with a fringe of yellow whiskers that almost matched Charlie's mane. They both lived in Tulip Hill Farm in Shropshire, England. Mister Spinks and everyone else thought Charlie was too old to work. Everyone, that is, except Charlie. He had reached the great age of twenty-eight, but in spite of his years and his dignity, he could still roll over. Not just half way, but a complete once over! It was tremendous to behold. And when his

rheumatism didn't bother him, he kicked and capered like any frisky colt. Mister Spinks was a tough yet tender man. He thought a lot of Charlie, who had been a strong puller in his day. So he retired him and gave him a field all to himself, with a nice rain barrel for drinking water. Of course, it was a small field, and nothing much would grow on it, anyway. Nothing but nasty thistles and chickweed. Charlie despised them both. One was too prickly, the other too bitter. Quite regularly, Mister Spinks managed to bring him a wisp of hay, but even so, Charlie grew hungry and bored with his life.

He felt so useless. He missed the busyness of the old days: the plowing and the planting, the logging and hauling, the raking and the reaping. And he had nowhere

at all to go. Not to the millhouse to grind the grain. Nor to the greengrocer's to deliver parsnips and peas and potatoes. Nor to the blacksmith for a new set of shoes. Not even to the old Boar's Head Inn on Cowcross Road. Perhaps what happened at the Boar's Head was what he missed most of all. Charlie remembered how every afternoon at the stroke of five Birdie would appear. She was not a bird at all; she was a plump cook in a white apron. She would bounce out of the inn like a cuckoo from a clock. Then she would pull a stout rope beside the door, which set a bell to ringing. This meant that the apple tarts were nicely browned and ready to come out of the oven. Quick as flies the people would come swarming. There were teamsters and tailors, carpenters and cobblers, bankers and barristers, goldsmiths, silversmiths, and blacksmiths. They came afoot, they came on wagons, they came in fine carriages. In the courtyard they separated. Some went indoors, and the others gathered at the swing-out, swing-in window to the kitchen.

Mister Spinks was one who went inside; he enjoyed a bumper of punch with his apple tart. Charlie was always left standing at the hitching rail with the lines wrapped loosely around it. He towered above the elegant little hackneys and the workaday cobs. The moment Mister Spinks disappeared, Charlie used to pull the lines free and lumber over to the swing-in, swing-out window. There he would wait politely while the two-legged creatures were served. They all slapped him affectionately on the rump as they went back to their carriages. Then at last it would be Charlie's turn. His nostrils would flutter in excitement as Birdie held out the flat of her hand. On it there was always a beautiful apple tart, oozing with juices that smelled of sugar and spices. "Charlie, you rascal!" She would exclaim. "Now you get back to the hitching rail and do your eating there. I don't want you slobbering all over my clean window."

When Mister Spinks finally came out, wiping his whiskers on his sleeve, he never seemed to notice that Charlie's lines were no longer wrapped about the rail. He just hooked him up, climbed onto the seat of the wagon, gave a "cluck-cluck" to Charlie, and off they would go, home to Tulip Hill.

In his retirement, Charlie sadly missed this five o'clock treat. He felt hungry and forlorn in his silent field with only the grasshoppers thrumming their wings together, and a woodpecker drilling holes in an old dead tree. Morning, noon, and night were all alike. It was a world of nothing but weeds and sky. Day by day, his head dropped lower and his tail hung limp as an old rope. A month dragged by. Then, late one afternoon, a curious thing happened. Charlie was aroused from his daydreaming by the wind. It was blowing sharply, bringing city smells and city sounds. He lifted his head, and suddenly the time clock in his mind began ringing. It was as if he heard a bell!

He had to answer it. He trotted across the field, around the old dead tree, past the water barrel, faster and faster until he broke into a gallop. He was heading straight for the fence, he was going to jump it! With all his strength and power, he collected his great bulk and flung himself up and over, but he was traveling too fast. His forefeet struck the top rail, smashing it to bits. He didn't even feel or hear the crash. He was over! He was free! In a burst he was down the lane and out upon the pike, galumphing toward the village. His feathers swished. His hoofs clanked. Kal-lop, kal-lop, kal-lippity-klop. Stately and bold and full of purpose he trotted around the bend, down through a gap in the hills, past the old steepled church, and into

Cowcross Road. It was just like the old days! There was the friendly Boar's Head Inn and the same jolly people gathering at the window. They seemed delighted to see him and thumped him more affectionately than ever. "Let's give first place to Charlie," one said. And they all bowed and made way for him. When he reached the swing-out, swing-in window, he bunted it with his nose and came face-to-face with Birdie. Eeeek! She almost dropped the plate of apple tarts.

"Charlie!" she cried. "Charlie, Charlie!" and she reached up and kissed him on his nose. Then she chose the biggest, brownest, juiciest tart of all for him. And she let him eat it right there at the window. It was better than old times! There was no waiting in line, no wagon to pull. Charlie hadn't been so happy in weeks. He

trumpeted his joy to the people. Then with a snort of greeting to the unfortunate horses tied at the rail, he galumphed back home at an easy gait, the feathers on his feet swinging in the little breeze he made. He felt young and frisky again, and his loneliness vanished like a fog when the sun comes out.

Each day now, he trotted to the inn and arrived before five o'clock. And each day, he bunted the swing-out, swing-in window and poked his nose into the kitchen. If the kettle was hissing or the dishes making a clatter, he let out a lusty bugle to make Birdie notice him. She always jumped and grabbed herself as if an icicle had dropped down her dress. "Lor-love-a duck!" she exclaimed, "It must be time to ring the bell. Whatever would I do without you, Charlie?" And she bounced out of the inn like a cuckoo from the clock. And soon the bell was binging and bonging, and farmers' wagons were pulling up, and fine carriages were all about, and people were swarming into the inn for their apple tarts and tea.

Slowly, a beautiful thing was happening to Charlie. Birdie began depending more and more on him to remind her when it was teatime. He became her alarm clock.

Then something even more wonderful happened. She taught him how to take the rope between his big yellow teeth and ring the bell himself! At last something important to do! Every day. Rain or shine. Summer or winter.

Of course, Mister Spinks heard about these daily jaunts. The news traveled to Tulip Hill and well beyond. And one afternoon as he was sauntering into the Boar's Head, he caught sight of Charlie, large as life, over at the window. He fancied for a moment the thought of speaking to Charlie, but he couldn't quite bring himself to do it. He just gave a wink in his direction; then, chuckling, he quickly turned his head, pretending not to see. It was kind of a shared secret. In the course of time, Mister Spinks's wife noticed the broken fence rail and chided him about fixing it, but he never seemed to get around to it, so he never did fix that fence.

美女牌香
穉英

The Horse

BY ELIZABETH MADOX ROBERTS

His bridle hung
around the post;
The sun and leaves made spots come down;
I looked close at him through the fence;
The post was drab and he was brown.

His nose was long and hard and still,
And on his lip were specks like chalk.
But once he opened his eyes;
And he began to talk.

He didn't talk out with his mouth;
He didn't talk with words or noise.
The talk was there along his nose;
It seemed and then it was.

He said that drab was just about
The same as brown, but he was not
A post, he said, to hold a fence.
"I'm horse," he said, "that's what!"

And then he shut his eyes again,
As still as they had been before.
He said for me to run along
And not to bother him anymore.

Wild Horses

BY MARY CROW

But every night now
for a month
I have run away
to the blue lake
where the wild horses
come to drink . . .

. . . In the moonlight
the white coats are blue
and the bays are shadows
I stand perfectly still.
My legs grow long and powerful.
I will run with the horses.

Happy Horsemanship

(An excerpt from "Let's Get Ready!" chapter)

BY DOROTHY HENDERSON PINCH

**Horses
are
something
to
dream
about**

**and
to
wish
for.**

ALWAYS APPROACH ME FROM my near (left) side, if you can. This is the side from which I am led, tacked and untacked, and mounted and dismounted, as well. Always walk (don't run!) quietly toward me. It is better to move toward my neck, rather than go directly to my head. (Sometimes I will jump away if a hand is suddenly raised to my face.) It is always wise to say a few words to me as you approach from any direction. A kind but firm voice will tell me you are a friend that I can trust; I might be frightened or upset by a loud, rough voice. It is most important to speak to me if you must approach me from the rear. When I hear your voice, I will know that you are coming, but otherwise I might be startled and kick first, then look around afterward. Don't put a hand unexpectedly upon my hindquarters! I may be surprised and kick. Anytime it is necessary to touch my hindquarters, put your hand on my neck or shoulder first, and move it slowly back over my body, speaking to me at the same time. Then I will know what is touching me and will not be surprised or frightened.

If you need to go from one side of me to the other, pass in front of me or under my neck, if possible. Otherwise, go far enough behind me to be well out of reach of my heels. When I am loose in my stall, which is my room in the stable, or out to eat grass in my pasture, I usually wear a halter, with which I can be led or tied. Sometimes it is hung outside my stall, ready for use. The proper piece of equipment with which to lead me is called a leadshank. As I like to chew on leather, the part near my mouth is made of chain links—which spoils all my fun! Lead me from my near side, walking by my head or with me a little behind you.

Don't let me get in front of you or with my head turned toward the right. In either of these positions, I can be difficult to control and may even get away from you! Hold the leadshank in your right hand about six inches from my head. Be sure not to let the extra length dangle on the ground, where it might be trampled or tangled around your legs! Fold the loose end in the palm of your left hand. (Never wrap it around your hand: if I started to run, you would be caught and dragged after me.)

When leading me, look in the direction in which you are going and walk forward; usually I will come with you without any urging. If I do not start immediately, or lag back, don't try to pull me after you. I can—and will—outpull you anytime!

Bring me forward with little tugs on the leadshank; I don't resist that kind of pressure. Do not look back at me except when you lead me through narrow places, such as gates or doorways. Then always watch carefully that I enter the opening straight and do not strike my hips. (The point of my hip is like your elbow—the bone is right under the skin with no flesh to protect it, so if it strikes a post or doorjamb I can be painfully injured. Ouch!) To steer me while leading: a tug on the leadshank will direct my head toward the left, the firm pressure of your shoulder or elbow against my neck will move me toward the right. To slow down or stop—again, short tugs instead of a steady pull. And always remember to let me know what you want. (A firm, commanding "whoa!" will mean "stop" to me.)

Always groom me before I am ridden. Grooming is the way you keep me clean. These are the tools used for this purpose; together they are called my grooming kit. Put my grooming kit in a box or basket with a handle. This makes it easy to carry and store the tools:

- The hoof pick—for cleaning out the feet.
- The *dandy brush*—for removing heavy dirt, caked mud, and sweat from my coat.
- The *body brush*—to remove dust and scurf from my coat, mane, and tail.
- The *currycomb*—for cleaning the body brush.
- The *water brush*—to use damp, on my mane, tail, legs, and feet.
- The *stable sponge*—for cleaning eyes, nostrils, lips, dock, and for body bathing.
- The *stable rubber*—for a final polish after grooming.
- The *sweat scraper*—to remove sweat and water from the coat.

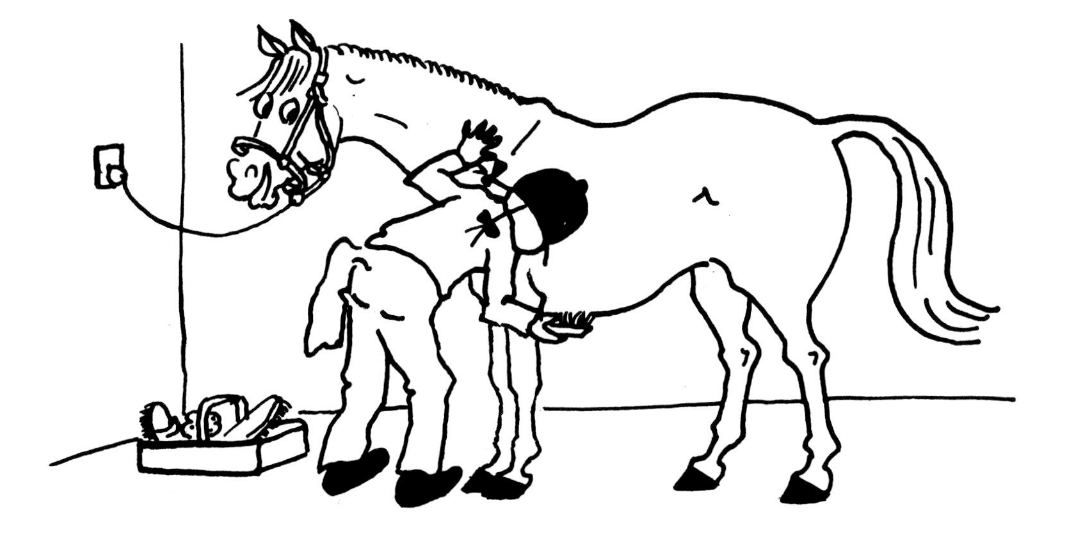

When you are ready to groom me, bring my grooming kit, and a bucket of water as well. Fasten me by my halter with a rope that is short enough to keep me from reaching around and nipping you. Remember, I have ticklish spots, and if I am touched on one of these places while you are grooming me, the only way I can show my annoyance is by a nip or a kick. Behind the elbows, under the belly, and the flank in front of the hip may be sensitive spots, so brush carefully and watch my teeth and heels!

Pick up each hoof in turn; remove whatever may be lodged in the foot with the point of the hoof pick, working downward from heel to toe.

Now the dandy brush may be used, beginning at the poll on the near side and working toward the tail. This stiff, long-bristled brush may be used in either hand in short, sweeping motions, drawn briskly through the hair. It is especially useful for removing sweat marks from the saddle region, and caked dirt from the belly and points of the hocks, fetlocks, and pasterns. (It is best not to use this stiff brush on the more tender parts of my body.) When working on my hind legs, hold my tail in your free hand. (This often discourages me from kicking.)

Next, use the body brush to groom my entire body. Its soft bristles are used in short, circular strokes in the direction of the lay of my coat. It can be used comfortably on my entire body, including my head.

The hand nearest the head holds the body brush, and the currycomb is held in the other hand. After four or five strokes, draw the brush smartly across the teeth of the currycomb to dislodge the dirt. (The currycomb is cleaned by tapping it on the floor.)

To do my mane, first throw it over the wrong side of my neck and brush the crest. Bring it back to the right side and brush a few locks at a time. Brush the ends first to remove the tangles, then work toward the roots.

My tail is cared for in the same manner. Hold the tail to one side (don't stand behind me!) and shake out a few locks at a time. Your hand firmly holding the hair between my dock and the tangle you are unsnarling spares me any discomfort.

The sponge cleanses my eyes, nostrils, lips, and under my dock. (It is used also to bathe the sweat from under my saddle and bridle after I have been ridden on a warm day or to bathe my entire body if I have become overheated in the hot weather. Tepid water, with liniment added, is used for this bathing.)

The sweat scraper is drawn over the coat in the direction of hair growth to free it of sweat or wash water.

The soft end hairs of the water brush, dipped in a bucket with the excess water squeezed out against the edge, are used to dampen my mane and keep it smooth. Start at the roots and brush downward. This brush may be used to put a finishing touch on the top of my tail and legs as well. Last of all, use the stable rubber, folded, to polish my coat after the cleansing tools have been used. Now I am spic-and-span—and ready to be saddled.

When you ride me, I wear a bridle, a saddle, and sometimes a martingale. Together, these are called my tack, just as your coat, hat, shoes, etc. are called your clothes. They are kept in a tackroom. I am said to be tacked up or untacked.

My bridle and martingale help you to manage me. My saddle makes it easier for you to stay on my back, and a lot more comfortable, too! A bridle is made of leather, with a metal bit. I wear the bridle on my head, with the bit in my mouth. The reins, which you will be holding in your hands, are attached to this bit, so through them you can create different pressures on the sensitive bars of my jaw.

White Horses

BY ELEANOR FARJEON

Count the white horses you meet on the way,
Count the white horses, child, day after day.
Keep a wish ready for wishing—if you
Wish on the ninth horse, your wish will come true.

I saw a white horse at the end of the lane,
I saw a white horse canter down by the shore,
I saw a white horse that was drawing a wain,
And one drinking out of a trough: that made four.

I saw a white horse gallop over the down,
I saw a white horse looking over a gate,
I saw a white horse on the way into town,
And one on the way coming back: that made eight.

But oh for the ninth one: where he tossed his mane,
And cantered and galloped and whinnied and swished
His silky white tail, I went looking in vain,
And the wish I had ready could never be wished.

Count the white horses you meet on the way,
Count the white horses, child, day after day.
Keep a wish ready for wishing—if you
Wish on the ninth horse, your wish will come true.

Thoroughbreds and Their Mascots

BY C. W. ANDERSON

ALMOST ALL THOROUGHBREDS HAVE a pronounced liking for some animal around the stable, and sometimes this affection is hard to understand. If it's another horse, then it is usually a stable pony that will be his favorite companion—and almost invariably the commonest, plainest one. There is no snobbishness among Thoroughbreds. Many of the blue bloods of the turf choose very strange friends. As a rule, dogs rank first in favor. The great Omaha had a little terrier named Rags as his mascot. Bold Venture, winner of Derby and Preakness, had a Boston bull that was always with him in the stable and traveled in his stall in the private car that took him to Kentucky. An understanding between horses and dogs is age-old and to be expected, but it's hard to account for the fact that the champion Cavalcade had a stuffed dog that he always liked to have in his stall.

Very often a chicken or rooster will be a racehorse's friend, sometimes to such an extent that the horse will let him sit on his back or withers and live in his stall.

Goats are always popular around a stable, and it is rare that one ever is kicked, even though they run around the legs of excitable Thoroughbreds. The more placid an animal is, the more certain it seems that the highest strung Thoroughbred will prefer his companionship.

One racehorse had a parrot for a mascot. The parrot lived in his stall and usually perched on the horse's back. He always rode out to the track and sat on the rail, screaming, as the horse galloped by. Whether the parrot was cheering the horse on or not is hard to say, but the owner said that both animals were unhappy when separated. If a horse shows a fondness for any animal, no matter how strange the companionship may seem, it is encouraged by the trainer. There have been many instances of horses who lost their winning form when separated from a mascot, so trainers always indulge any whim of their charges in this direction. A complete list of mascots of Thoroughbreds would include almost all domestic animals, occasionally even human beings.

The Horse and His Boy

(An excerpt from "How Shasta Set Out on His Travels" chapter)

BY C. S. LEWIS

"OH HURRAH!" SAID SHASTA. "Then we'll go North. I've been longing to go to the North all my life."

"Of course you have," said the Horse. "That's because of the blood that's in you. I'm sure you're true Northern stock. But not too loud. I should think they'd be asleep soon now."

"I'd better creep back and see," suggested Shasta.

"That's a good idea," said the Horse. "But take care you're not caught."

It was a good deal darker now and very silent except for the sound of the waves on the beach, which Shasta hardly noticed because he had been hearing it day and night as long as he could remember. The cottage, as he approached it, showed no light. When he listened at the front, there was no noise. When he went round to the only window, he could hear, after a second or two, the familiar noise of the old fisherman's squeaky snore. It was funny to think that if all went well he would never hear it again. Holding his breath and feeling a little bit sorry, but much less sorry than he was glad, Shasta glided away over the grass and went to the donkey's stable, groped along to a place he knew where the key was hidden, opened the door, and found the Horse's saddle and bridle, which had been locked up there for the night. He bent forward and kissed the donkey's nose. "I'm sorry we can't take you," he said.

"There you are at last," said the Horse when he got back to it. "I was beginning to wonder what had become of you."

"I was getting your things out of the stable," replied Shasta. "And now, can you tell me how to put them on?"

For the next few minutes Shasta was at work, very cautiously to avoid jingling, while the Horse said things like, "Get that girth a bit tighter," or "You'll find a buckle lower down," or "You'll need to shorten those stirrups a good bit." When all was finished it said: "Now, we've got to have reins for the look of the thing, but you won't be using them. Tie them to the saddle-bow: very slack so that I can do what I like with my head. And, remember—you are not to touch them."

"What are they for, then?" asked Shasta.

"Ordinarily, they are for directing me," replied the Horse. "But as I intend to do all the directing on this journey, you'll please keep your hands to yourself. And there's another thing. I'm not going to have you grabbing my mane."

"But I say," pleaded Shasta. "If I'm not to hold on by the reins or by your mane, what am I to hold on by?"

"You hold on with your knees," said the Horse. "That's the secret of good riding. Grip my body between your knees as hard as you like; sit straight up, straight as a poker; keep your elbows in. And by the way, what did you do with the spurs?"

"Put them on my heels, of course," said Shasta. "I do know that much."

"Then you can take them off and put them in the saddlebag. We may be able to sell them when we get to Tashbaan. Ready? And now I think you can get up."

"Ooh! You're a dreadful height," gasped Shasta after his first, and unsuccessful, attempt.

"I'm a horse, that's all," was the reply. "Anyone would think I was a haystack from the way you're trying to climb up me! There, that's better. Now sit up, and remember what I told you about your knees. Funny to think of me who has led cavalry charges and won races having a potato sack like you in the saddle! However, off we go." It chuckled, not unkindly.

And it certainly began their night journey with great caution. First of all, it went just south of the fisherman's cottage to the little river, which there ran into the sea, and took care to leave in the mud some very plain hoof-marks pointing South. But as soon as they were in the middle of the ford, it turned upstream and waded till they were about a hundred yards farther inland than the cottage. Then it selected a nice gravelly bit of bank, which would take no footprints, and came out on the Northern side. Then, still at a walking pace, it went Northward till the cottage, the one tree, the donkey's stable, and the creek—everything, in fact, that Shasta had ever known—had sunk out of sight in the gray summer-night darkness. They had been going uphill and now were at the top of the ridge—that ridge that had always been the boundary of Shasta's known world. He could not see what was ahead except that it was all open and grassy. It looked endless: wild and lonely and free.

"I say!" observed the Horse. "What a place for a gallop, eh!"

"Oh don't let's," said Shasta. "Not yet. I don't know how to—please, Horse. I don't know your name."

"Breehy-hinny-brinny-hooky-hah," said the Horse.

"I'll never be able to say that," said Shasta. "Can I call you Bree?"

"Well, if it's the best you can do, I suppose you must," said the Horse. "And what shall I call you?"

"I'm called Shasta."

"H'm," said Bree. "Well, now, there's a name that's really hard to pronounce. But now about this gallop. It's a good deal easier than trotting if you only knew, because you don't have to rise and fall. Grip with your knees and keep your eyes straight ahead between my ears. Don't look at the ground. If you think you're going to fall just grip harder and sit up straighter. Ready? Now: for Narnia and the North."

It was nearly noon on the following day when Shasta was wakened by something warm and soft moving over his face. He opened his eyes and found himself staring into the long face of a horse; its nose and lips were almost touching his. He remembered the exciting events of the previous night and sat up. But as he did so he groaned.

"Ow, Bree," he gasped. "I'm so sore. All over. I can hardly move."

"Good morning, small one," said Bree. "I was afraid you might feel a bit stiff. It can't be the falls. You didn't have more than a dozen or so, and it was all lovely, soft springy turf that must have been almost a pleasure to fall on. And the only one that might have been nasty was broken by that gorse bush. No: it's the riding itself that comes hard at first. What about breakfast? I've had mine."

"Oh bother breakfast. Bother everything," said Shasta. "I tell you I can't move." But the horse nuzzled at him with its nose and pawed him gently with a hoof till he had to get up. And then he looked about him and saw where they were. Behind them lay a little copse. Before them the turf, dotted with white flowers, sloped down to the brow of a cliff.

Far below them, so that the sound of the breaking waves was very faint, lay the sea. Shasta had never seen it from such a height and never seen so much of it before, nor dreamed how many colors it had. On either hand the coast stretched away, headland after headland, and at the points you could see the white foam running up the rocks but making no noise because it was so far off. There were gulls flying overhead, and the heat shivered on the ground; it was a blazing day. But what Shasta chiefly noticed was the air. He couldn't think what was missing, until at last he realized that there was no smell of fish in it. For, of course, neither in the cottage nor among the nets, had he ever been away from that smell in his life. And this new air was so delicious, and all his old life seemed so far away, that he forgot for a moment about his bruises and his aching muscles and said: "I say, Bree, didn't you say something about breakfast?"

"Yes, I did," answered Bree. "I think you'll find something in the saddlebags. They're over there on that tree where you hung them up last night—or early this morning, rather."

They investigated the saddlebags and the results were cheering—a meat pasty, only slightly stale, a lump of dried figs and another lump of green cheese, a little flask of wine, and some money, about forty crescents in all, which was more than Shasta had ever seen.

While Shasta sat down—painfully and cautiously—with his back against a tree and started on the pasty, Bree had a few more mouthfuls of grass to keep him company.

"Won't it be stealing to use the money?" asked Shasta.

"Oh," said the Horse, looking up with its mouth full of grass, "I never thought of that. A free horse and a talking horse mustn't steal, of course. But I think it's all right. We're prisoners and captives in enemy country. That money is booty, spoil. Besides, how are we to get any food for you without it? I suppose, like all humans, you won't eat natural food like grass and oats."

"I can't."

"Ever tried?"

"Yes, I have. I can't get it down at all. You couldn't either if you were me."

"You're rum little creatures, you humans," remarked Bree.

When Shasta had finished his breakfast (which was by far the nicest he had ever eaten), Bree said, "I think I'll have a nice roll before we put on that saddle again." And he proceeded to do so. "That's good. That's very good," he said, rubbing his back on the turf and waving all four legs in the air. "You ought to have one too, Shasta," he snorted. "It's most refreshing."

But Shasta burst out laughing and said, "You do look funny when you're on your back!"

"I look nothing of the sort," said Bree. But then suddenly he rolled round on his side, raised his head and looked hard at Shasta, blowing a little. "Does it really look funny?" he asked in an anxious voice.

"Yes, it does," replied Shasta. "But what does it matter?"

"You don't think, do you," said Bree, "that it might be a thing talking horses never do—a silly, clownish trick I've learned from the dumb ones? It would be dreadful to find, when I get back to Narnia, that I've picked up a lot of low, bad habits. What do you think, Shasta? Honestly, now. Don't spare my feelings. Should you think the real, free horses—the talking kind—do roll?"

"How should I know? Anyway, I don't think I should bother about it if I were you. We've got to get there first. Do you know the way?"

"I know my way to Tashbaan. After that comes the desert. Oh, we'll manage the desert somehow, never fear. Why, we'll be in sight of the Northern mountains then. Think of it! To Narnia and the North! Nothing will stop us then. But I'd be glad to be past Tashbaan. You and I are safer away from cities."

"Can't we avoid it?"

"Not without going a long way inland, and that would take us into cultivated land and main roads; and I wouldn't know the way. No, we'll just have to creep along the coast. Up here on the downs, we'll meet nothing but sheep and rabbits and gulls and a few shepherds. And by the way, what about starting?"

Shasta's legs ached terribly as he saddled Bree and climbed into the saddle, but the Horse was kindly to him and went at a soft pace all afternoon. When evening twilight came, they dropped by steep tracks into a valley and found a village. Before they got into it, Shasta dismounted and entered it on foot to buy a loaf and some onions and radishes. The Horse trotted round by the fields in the dusk and met Shasta at the far side. This became their regular plan every second night.

These were great days for Shasta, and every day better than the last as his muscles hardened and he fell less often. Even at the end of his training, Bree still said he sat like a bag of flour in the saddle. "And even if it was safe, young'un, I'd be ashamed to be seen with you on the main road."

But in spite of his rude words, Bree was a patient teacher. No one can teach riding so well as a horse. Shasta learned to trot, to canter, to jump, and to keep his seat even when Bree pulled up suddenly or swung unexpectedly to the left or the right—which, as Bree told him, was a thing you might have to do at any moment in a battle. And then, of course, Shasta begged to be told of the battles and wars in which Bree had carried the Tarkaan. And Bree would tell of forced marches and the fording of swift rivers, of charges and of fierce fights between cavalry and cavalry when the war horses fought as well as the men, being all fierce stallions, trained to bite and kick, and to rear at the right moment so that the horse's weight as well as the rider's would come down on an enemy's crest in the stroke of sword or battle-ax.

But Bree did not want to talk about the wars as often as Shasta wanted to hear about them. "Don't speak of them, youngster," he would say. "They were only the Tisroc's wars, and I fought in them as a slave and a dumb beast. Give me the Narnian wars, where I shall fight as a free Horse among my own people! Those will be wars worth talking about. Narnia and the North! Bra-ha-ha! Broo hoo!" Shasta soon learned, when he heard Bree talking like that, to prepare for a gallop.

Blackfoot Indian Legend of the Horse

AS TOLD BY HE-WHO-LOVES-HORSES

WHEN THE HORSES FIRST APPEARED to the Blackfeet people, they thought the strange animals were dogs sent as a gift from the sky from Old Man, creator of all things.

A long, long time ago we had to walk and walk from sky to sky, from camp to camp. Our dogs carried our rawhide bags and pulled our travois sleds. We walked so much that we wore out many moccasins going across the Plains.

All of a sudden, one day, coming from Old Man's sleeping room, west of the mountains, we saw some strange looking beasts. They were as big as elk and they had tails of straw. Lying across the backs of these beasts were two Kutani men. One beast was pulling a travois sled. We became afraid because we did not understand.

My best friend, Jumps-Over-the-Water, hid behind his mother's skirt. The bravest of all of us, known as Running Bear, ran behind the nearest tipi to hide. I was so frightened I could not move. I was away from the safety of my father's tipi. The men in our tribe yelled that we were not to be afraid—that we were the mighty Piegans who took the land away from the Kutani.

As I looked around, I saw that they were afraid. They all had big eyes and four of them had their hunting bows aimed. Then our chief Long Arrow laughed. He said, "These are from Old Man. They are a gift like the elk, antelope, buffalo, and bighorn sheep; they are called Sky Dogs."

Now, Long Arrow was very smart because he had walked around the Earth seven times from the Porcupine Hills down to the mouth of the Yellowstone. Everyone became quiet and trusted his knowledge. We waited for the Sky Dogs to reach our camp . . .

No one was afraid anymore. I went up to the smallest Sky Dog. I touched him gently from hoof to mane. I felt his soft, warm skin. He did not flicker. He did not move. I pressed my face close against his face. He still did not move. Long Arrow smiled at me and gave me the name He-Who-Loves-Horses.

Harper

Farewell to the Farm

BY ROBERT LOUIS STEVENSON

The coach is at the door at last;
The eager children, mounting fast
And kissing hands, in chorus sing:
Good-bye, good-bye, to everything!

To house and garden, field and lawn,
The meadow-gates we swung upon,
To pump and stable, tree and swing,
Good-bye, good-bye, to everything!

And fare you well forevermore,
O ladder at the hayloft door,
O hayloft where the cobwebs cling,
Good-bye, good-bye, to everything!

Crack goes the whip, and off we go;
The trees and houses smaller grow;
Last, round the woody turn we swing:
Good-bye, good-bye, to everything!

The Black Stallion

(An excerpt from "The Mystery Horse" chapter)

BY WALTER FARLEY

THE FOLLOWING NIGHT, WHEN Alec and Henry drove up to Belmont's main gate, they saw Joe's car parked there. Two men were inside. "That fellow with him must be Jim Neville," Alec said hopefully.

Henry brought the truck to a stop and lightly touched the horn. "Leave your car here," he called softly to Joe. "Jump on the truck—we've only a short way to go."

The two men climbed out of the car and leaped onto the truck's running board. Henry put the truck in gear as he saw Jake swing the gates open. Joe pushed his head in the open window near Henry. "Made it," he said. "Where do we go from here?"

"Hold tight, my friend. You'll find out," Henry said. Five minutes later, they came to a stop beside the track. Henry and Alec climbed out. A tall, broad-shouldered man stood beside Joe; his hat was shoved back off his forehead and Alec saw long streaks of gray running through his black hair. Somehow, Jim Neville looked just as Alec had imagined he would. Joe introduced them. After the introductions, Jim said, "Frankly," and his eyes squinted quizzically, "it's only the newspaperman in me that gets me out here tonight because, as much faith as I have in my pal Joe here, I can't imagine any horse in racing—today anyway—that can match strides with Cyclone or Sun Raider!"

Henry smiled. "Sure," he said, "I'd say the same thing if I hadn't seen the Black run!"

Jim Neville looked questioningly at Henry. "Say, you're not by any chance the same Henry Dailey who rode Chang to victory in all those races about twenty years ago, are you?"

"Sure he is!" Alec said proudly. Jim Neville pulled his hat down over his forehead. Alec could see that once again he was the reporter on the scent of a story.

"And you believe," Jim said seriously, "that you've got a horse here that can beat both Sun Raider and Cyclone?"

"Yep," Henry answered. "It's Alec's horse; I just help train him."

Joe Russo spoke up. "Why not show him the Black, Henry, and then we'll let him draw his own conclusions?"

"Good idea," said Alec, as he walked toward the back of the truck. He led the Black out on the ramp.

"Say," he heard Jim exclaim, "he is a giant of a horse!" The stallion shook his head. He was full of life tonight for he knew well that he was going to run. His small, savagely beautiful head turned toward the group of men below him. He drew up, made a single effort to jump, which Alec curbed, and then stood quivering while the boy talked soothingly and patted him. Jake came up and Henry introduced him to Joe and Jim.

"Say," Jake smiled, "this is growin' into quite a shindig, isn't it?"

Jim walked carefully around the stallion. "Watch out. He might kick, if you get too close," warned Alec. "He doesn't know you."

"Don't worry! I won't get too close to this fellow," Jim said. I'm beginning to see what you fellows mean," he added. "If he can run as well as he looks—" Henry disappeared into the truck and came out leading Napoleon. "Hey, what've you got here, another champion?" Jim threw back his head and howled.

"This is Napoleon." Henry grinned.

"He has sort of a quieting effect on the Black, so we always bring him along," Alec explained.

Jim Neville watched as Napoleon reached his nose up toward the stallion's. "Maybe not such a bad idea, after all," he said.

A few minutes later, they boosted Alec into the saddle. The Black pawed the ground. Jim Neville got too close and the Black's teeth snapped as he tried to reach him. Henry held him back. It was plain to see he wasn't used to seeing so many people around at one time. He tossed his head up and down, his heavy mane falling over his forehead. Suddenly, he rose on his hind legs, tearing the bridle out of Henry's grasp; his legs struck out, hitting Henry in the arm. Alec pulled hard on the reins and jerked him to the side. "Black!" he said. "Down!" The men retreated quickly to a safe distance. Jake was rolling up Henry's sleeve, which was wet with blood.

"Did he get you bad, Henry?" Alec asked. Jake and Henry were inspecting the wound.

"Nothing broke," answered Jake.

"Just a bad cut; we'll go up to the First Aid Room and fix it!"

"No, we won't," Henry said. "I came down here to watch this workout, and I'm going to see it. I'll take care of this later; you gotta take more'n a cut in this business."

"He sure is a devil!" Jim Neville yelled from the other side of the Black.

"We got him excited, that's all," answered Henry. "First time he's done that to me."

Again the stallion reared and Alec brought him down. "I'll get him out on the track, kid," Jake yelled. The Black pranced nervously as they went through the gate.

Once again, Alec felt his body grow warm with excitement. He patted the crest on the stallion's neck. "We're off, fella," he said.

Alec looked back at the small group of men behind him. They were all leaning on the fence, watching eagerly. Joe Russo's voice drifted toward him. "That kid's not going on any picnic," he said. Alec grasped the reins still tighter and leaned over until his head touched the stallion's. He knew full well the danger that was his every time he rode the Black, especially when he let him loose on the track. The stallion would never hurt him knowingly, but once he got his head he was no longer the Black that Alec knew—but once again a wild stallion that had never been clearly broken, and never would be!

Suddenly, the Black bolted. His action shifted marvelously as his powerful legs swept over the ground. Fleet hoofbeats made a clattering roar in Alec's ears. The stallion's speed became greater and greater. Alec's body grew numb, the terrific speed made it hard for him to breathe. Once again, the track became a blur, and he was conscious only of the endless white fence slipping by. His fingers grasped the stallion's mane and his head hung low beside his neck. His only thought was to remain on the Black's back and to stay alert. His breath came in short gasps, the white fence faded from his vision; desperately, he tried to open his eyes, but his lids seemed held down by weights. Bells began to ring in his ears. Alec's fingers tightened on the Black's mane. He lost all track of time—then the world started turning upside down. It seemed hours later that he felt arms reach around his waist. Then, the next thing he knew, he found himself lying flat on his back beside the truck. He looked up at the men grouped around him. Henry knelt beside him, his white handkerchief stained with large dark spots bulging around his arm. Alec's eyes fell to his own hands. Strands of long, black hair were clenched between doubled fists. Questioningly, he looked up at Henry. "How—" he began.

"It's all right, kid. You wouldn't let go of him. Feel all right?"

"Kinda dizzy," answered Alec.

"Where's the Black?"

"He's okay—we put him in the truck with Napoleon."

"Did I fall off, Henry?" Alec asked.

Jake's high-pitched voice reached Alec's ears. "Fall off?" he said. "Boy, if that hoss was still running, you'd still be on him. Took all of us to get you off his back when he did stop, and then Henry was the only one of us who could get near him."

"I'm glad I stuck on him," Alec said. "Y'know, Henry, we've never seen that horse run his fastest yet. I just couldn't seem to breathe that time."

"Takes courage to ride him, kid," Henry answered. "I'm pretty proud of you, but let's try getting you to your feet. Better for you if you can walk around." Alec swayed a little as Henry and Jake lifted him up, but gradually the earth stopped turning around and his brain cleared. He breathed in the night air deeply.

Jim Neville came up. "Kid," he said, "I've seen a lot of riding in my day, but never any to equal that!"

Jim then turned to Henry. "You were right, Mr. Dailey—he is the fastest horse we've ever seen. I can hardly believe what I saw with my own eyes but"—Jim held the face of a stopwatch up in front of Henry—"I can't deny this!"

Then he turned brusquely to Joe Russo. "And now, Joe, we both have a deadline to make, so let's get going."

"Right, Jim."

"Come around again—anytime you want," Henry urged, "and we'll let you see the grandest animal on four feet run without even charging admission."

Jim Neville's eyes twinkled. "A lot of people are going to see that horse in action if I have anything to say about it!" he said.

Alec felt the earth whirl around him again. "Honest, Jim," he said, "do you think we could?"

"I'm not promising anything, kid," replied Jim, "but I'm going to start something or I miss my guess. Take a look at my column tomorrow. And now we do have to get going. Come on, Joe."

"I'll go along with you and let you out," said Jake. After they had gone, Henry put his arm through Alec's and they walked back and forth until the blood once again was circulating through the boy's legs.

"I feel okay now, Henry," he said. They climbed into the truck. Alec looked back through the small window and saw the stallion peering anxiously at him. "Yep, mister," he said, "that was quite a ride!"

"Well, Alec," Henry said, "I hope that whatever Jim Neville is going to do gets us in that race. You're not hoping any more than I am."

The next day was Saturday. Alec rushed over to the barn immediately after breakfast. Henry always had a morning paper, and probably he was already

reading Jim Neville's column. Sure enough, he was sitting outside reading as Alec came up.

"What's he say?" the boy asked anxiously.

Henry grinned as he handed him the paper. "Read it for yourself."

Alec's eyes swept over the headline—"Who Is the Mystery Horse That Can Beat Both Cyclone and Sun Raider?" "Yes, I know," Jim Neville wrote. "I'm the guy that said there wasn't a horse in the world that could beat that rarin' red bundle of dynamite—Cyclone. Not even Sun Raider. Yep, and I'm the guy that wrote to Messrs. Volence and Hurst, owners of these Thoroughbreds, suggesting the coming match between their horses on the twenty-sixth of June—just two weeks off.

"This race in my mind—and I suppose in the minds of the whole American public—was to settle one thing: to see which horse was the fastest in the country! Both Cyclone and Sun Raider had beaten everything they had met on the track, and it was only natural then that they should meet to settle this question of track supremacy.

"But now, in my mind, this race will no longer prove who's the fastest horse on four legs because I've seen a horse that can beat both of them. This is something I have to get off my chest because you racing fans are going to crown the winner of Chicago's match race as the world's fastest horse—and it isn't true. There is still another horse—a great horse, who can beat either one of them.

"It's only fair to tell you that this horse has never raced on a track, and perhaps never will—because he lacks the necessary registration papers. And now I find that I'm coming to the end of my column, so I'll close with just this reminder that while you folks are acclaiming the winner of the coming Cyclone–Sun Raider race as today's champion, I know of a horse—a mystery horse that's right here in New York—who could probably make both of them eat his dust!"

"Say, that is starting something," said Alec.

"You said it, son; he'll have everybody on his neck before this day is out!"

"He didn't come right out and suggest that the Black run in the match race, though, Henry," Alec said.

"No—but he's left the door wide open, and you can bet somebody will suggest it."

"Gee, I hope it works, Henry. Just think, the Black against Cyclone and Sun Raider. Boy! What a race!"

"You said it!" Henry agreed. Then he paused for a minute. "Say, Alec, wonder if we did get the Black in the race, how do you think your folks would take it? About you riding, I mean."

Alec's eyes met Henry's. "They just gotta let me ride, Henry. They'll understand, I'm sure, especially after we tell them how I've been riding the Black at Belmont. Funny thing, Henry, Mother decided last night that she's going to Chicago middle of next week to visit my aunt for a couple of weeks. She'll be there at the same time as the match race!"

"Whew," said Henry, "that's somethin'!"

"Mother isn't interested in races; she probably won't even go to see it! You know, Henry, as long as we don't even know yet whether the Black is going to be in the race, I won't even mention it to Mother. If the Black does get in, I'll talk it all over with Dad; he'll understand."

"Hope so," answered Henry.

When Alec looked over the evening papers that night, he saw that Henry certainly was right about everybody's jumping on Jim Neville's neck. The sports pages were filled with articles ridiculing Jim's "insane idea" that there was a horse in America—yes, right here in New York—that could beat the two champions! Because Jim Neville's column was carried in papers from coast to coast, and because he was one of the foremost sports authorities in the country, his articles on the mystery horse aroused more and more curiosity with every day that passed.

And in spite of the criticism that he was getting, Jim wouldn't let the public forget about his mystery horse. Each day in his column, he would carry a paragraph about him. Each night on his network sports program, he would again mention him. One sports writer wrote, "Only a figure as well-known as Jim Neville could have created such a hullabaloo as is now going on over the merits of a mystery horse that Neville claims can beat both Sun Raider and Cyclone!"

A week passed, and the small snowball that Jim had started rolling continued to gain momentum. "Who is this mystery horse?" the racing public wanted to know.

Jim's only reply was that he had promised to keep his name a secret, but that he could get him at a moment's notice. He called Henry and Alec on the telephone. "Don't run him at Belmont any more," he told them. "This is getting bigger than I had even hoped it would. We'll have the Black in that race yet!"

A Short History of the Cowboy

BY HOLLING C. HOLLING

THERE WERE NO CATTLE in North America (except buffalo and the Arctic musk oxen), until the Spaniards came over, and the Indians had never seen horses. The Spaniards brought horses and cattle, burros and hogs to Mexico, and later, when they moved into New Mexico and Texas, the animals came, too.

Some of these animals got separated from the herds and grew up wild. Over a period of three hundred years, the horses, cattle, burros, and hogs (which later were called razorbacks) multiplied until there were great numbers. The wild cattle, because they developed long horns on the open plains of Texas, later became known as Texas longhorns.

The wild horses were known as mustangs, from a Spanish word meaning "wild" or "strayed." Soon, anyone could have cattle and horses in this country because all they had to do was to go out and catch them.

The Mexican people were the first cowboys. They were called *vaqueros*. To catch their animals, they used a rope, which they called *la reata*. We have shortened this to reata and lariat.

They used also a peculiar type of saddle with a big horn in front. Later on, Americans wandered down into this Southwest country and copied the ways of the Mexicans. They built *ranchos*, which we call ranches. Americans also used ropes and saddles and spurs, copied from the Mexican vaqueros. Eventually, this land became part of the United States and was divided into the states that now form the northern boundary of Mexico—California, Arizona, New Mexico, and Texas. All the Mexicans living here became Americans, though many of them still speak Spanish.

So you see, cattle and horses came from Spain originally, and the science of the cowboys was developed among the Mexicans.

Winter's Tale

(An excerpt from "A White Horse Escapes" chapter)

BY MARK HELPRIN

THERE WAS A WHITE horse, on a quiet winter morning when snow covered the streets gently and was not deep, and the sky was swept with vibrant stars, except in the east, where dawn was beginning in a light blue flood. The air was motionless but would soon start to move as the sun came up and winds from Canada came charging down the Hudson.

The horse had escaped from his master's small clapboard stable in Brooklyn. He trotted alone over the carriage road of the Williamsburg Bridge, before the light, while the toll keeper was sleeping by his stove and many stars were still blazing above the city. Fresh snow on the bridge muffled his hoofbeats, and he sometimes turned his head and looked behind him to see if he was being followed. He was warm from his own effort and he breathed steadily, having loped four or five miles through the dead of Brooklyn past silent churches and shuttered stores. Far to the south, in the black, ice-choked waters of the Narrows, a sparkling light marked the ferry on its way to Manhattan, where only market men were up, waiting for the fishing boats to glide down through Hell Gate and the night.

The horse was crazy, but, still, he was able to worry about what he had done. He knew that shortly his master and mistress would arise and light the fire. Utterly humiliated, the cat would be tossed out the kitchen door, to fly backward into a snow-covered sawdust pile. The scent of blueberries and hot batter would mix with the sweet smell of a pine fire, and not too long afterward his master would stride across the yard to the stable to feed him and hitch him up to the milk wagon. But he would not be there.

This was a good joke, this defiance, which made his heart beat in terror, for he was sure his master would soon be after him. Though he realized that he might be subject to a painful beating, he sensed that the master was amused, pleased, and touched by rebellion as often as not—if it were in the proper form and done well, courageously. A shapeless, coarse revolt (such as kicking down the stable door) would occasion the whip. But not even then would the master always use it, because he prized a spirited animal, and he knew of and was grateful for the mysterious intelligence of this white horse, an intelligence that even he could not ignore except at his peril and to his sadness. Besides, he loved the horse and did not really mind the chase through Manhattan (where the horse always went), since it afforded him the chance to enlist old friends in the search and the opportunity of visiting a great number of saloons where he would inquire, over a beer or two, if anyone had seen his enormous and beautiful white stallion rambling about in the nude, without bit, bridle, or blanket.

The horse could not do without Manhattan. It drew him like a magnet, like a vacuum, like oats, or a mare, or an open, never-ending, tree-lined road. He came off the bridge ramp and stopped short. A thousand streets lay before him, silent but for the sound of the gemlike wind. Driven with snow, white and empty, they were a maze for his delight as the newly arisen wind whistled across still untouched drifts and rills. He passed empty theaters, counting houses, and forested wharves where the snow-lined spars looked like long black groves of pine. He passed dark factories and deserted parks, and rows of little houses where wood just fired filled the air with sweet reassurance. He passed the frightening common cellars full of ragpickers and men without limbs. The door of a market bar was flung open momentarily for a torrent of boiling water that splashed over the street in a cloud of steam. Sleds and wagons began to radiate from the markets, alive with the pull of their stocky dray horses, racing up the main streets, ringing bells. But he kept away from the markets, because there it was noontime even at dawn, and he followed the silent tributaries of the main streets, passing the exposed steelwork of buildings in the intermission of feverish construction. And he was seldom out of sight of the new bridges, which had married beautiful womanly Brooklyn to her rich uncle, Manhattan; had put the city's hand out to the country; and were the end of the past because they spanned not only distance and deep water but dreams and time.

The tail of the white horse swished back and forth as he trotted briskly down empty avenues and boulevards. He moved like a dancer, which is not surprising: a horse is a beautiful animal, but it is perhaps most remarkable because it moves as if it always hears music. With a certainty that perplexed him, the white horse moved south toward the Battery, which was visible down a long narrow street as a

whitened field that was crossed by the long shadows of tall trees. By the Battery itself, the harbor took color with the new light, rocking in layers of green, silver, and blue. At the end of this polar rainbow, on the horizon, was a mass of white—the foil into which the entire city had been set—that was beginning to turn gold with the rising sun. The pale gold agitated in ascending waves of heat and refraction until it seemed to be a place of a thousand cities, or the border of heaven. The horse stopped to stare, his eyes filled with golden light. Steam issued from his nostrils as he stood in contemplation of the impossible and alluring distance. He stayed in the street as if he were a statue, while the gold strengthened and boiled before him in a bed of blue. It seemed to be a perfect place, and he determined to go there.

He started forward but soon found that the street was blocked by a massy iron gate that closed off the Battery. He doubled back and went another way, only to find another gate of exactly the same design. Trying many streets, he came to many heavy gates, none of which was open. While he was stuck in this labyrinth, the gold grew

in intensity and seemed to cover half the world. The empty white field was surely a way to that other, perfect world, and, though he had no idea of how he would cross the water, the horse wanted the Battery as if he had been born for it. He galloped desperately along the approachways, through the alleys, and over the snow-covered greens, always with an eye to the deepening gold.

At the end of what seemed to be the last street leading to the open, he found yet another gate, locked with a simple latch. He was breathing hard, and the condensed breath rose around his face as he stared through the bars. That was it: he would never step onto the Battery, there somehow to launch himself over the blue and green ribbons of water, toward the golden clouds. He was just about to turn and retrace his steps through the city, perhaps to find the bridge again and the way back to Brooklyn, when, in the silence that made his own breathing seem like the breaking of distant surf, he heard a great many footsteps.

At first they were faint, but they continued until they began to pound harder and harder and he could feel a slight trembling in the ground, as if another horse were going by. But this was no horse, these were men, who suddenly exploded into view. Through the black iron gate, he saw them running across the Battery. They took long high steps because the wind had drifted the snow almost up to their knees. Though they ran with all their strength, they ran in slow motion. It took them a long time to get to the center of the field, and when they did the horse could see that one man was in front and that the others, perhaps a dozen, chased him. The man being chased breathed heavily, and would sometimes drive ahead in deliberate bursts of speed. Sometimes he fell and bolted right back up, casting himself forward. They, too, fell at times, and got up more slowly. Soon this spread them out in a ragged line. They waved their arms and shouted. He, on the other hand, was perfectly silent, and he seemed almost stiff in his running, except when he leapt snowbanks or low rails and spread his arms like wings.

As the man got closer, the horse took a liking to him. He moved well, though not like a horse or a dancer or someone who always hears music, but with spirit. What was happening appeared to be, solely because of the way that this man moved, more profound than a simple chase across the snow. Nonetheless, they gained on him. It was difficult to understand how, since they were dressed in heavy coats and bowler hats, and he was hatless in a scarf and winter jacket. He had winter boots, and they had low street shoes, which had undoubtedly filled with numbing snow. But they were just as fast or faster than he was, they were good at it, and they seemed to have had much practice.

One of them stopped, spread his feet in the snow, raised a pistol in both hands, and fired at the fleeing man. The pistol crack echoed among the buildings facing the park and sent pigeons hurtling upward from the icy walks. The man in the lead looked back for a moment and then changed direction to cut in toward the streets, where the horse was standing mesmerized. They too changed course and gained on him even more as they ran the hypotenuse of a triangle and he ran its second leg. They were not more than two hundred feet from him when another dropped behind to fire. The sound was so close that the horse came alive and jumped back.

The man who was trying to escape approached the gate. The horse backed up behind a woodshed. He wanted no part of this. But, being too curious, he was unable to keep himself hidden for long, and he soon stuck his head around the corner of the shed to see what would happen. The fleeing man opened the gate with a violent uppercut, moved to the other side of it, and slammed it shut. He took a heavy steel dirk from his belt and breathlessly pounded the latch into an unmovable position. Then, with an agonized look, he turned and started up the street.

His pursuers were already at the fence when he slipped on a pool of ice. He went down hard, striking his head on the ground and tumbling over himself until he came to rest. The horse's heart was thundering as he saw the dozen men throw themselves at the fence, like a squad of soldiers. Their cruelty projected from them like sparks jumping a gap. One raised his pistol, but another—obviously their leader—said, "No! Not that way. We have him now. We'll do it slowly, with a knife." They started up the fence.

Had it not been for the horse peering at him from behind the woodshed, the downed man might have stayed down. His name was Peter Lake, and he said to himself out loud, "You're in bad shape when a horse takes pity on you, you stupid b—," which got him moving. He rose to his feet and addressed the horse. The twelve men, who couldn't see the horse standing behind the shed, thought that Peter Lake had gone mad or was playing a trick.

"Horse!" he called. The horse pulled back his head. "Horse!" shouted Peter Lake. "Please!" and he opened his arms. The other men began to drop to the near side of the fence. They were taking their time because they were only a few feet away, the street was deserted, he was not moving, and they were sure that they had him.

Peter Lake's heart beat so hard that it made his body jerk. He felt ridiculous and out of control, like an engine breaking itself apart.

"Oh Jesus," he said, vibrating like a mechanical toy, "Oh Jesus, Mary, and Joseph, send me an armored steamroller." Everything depended on the horse.

The horse bolted over the pool of ice toward Peter Lake and lowered his wide white neck. Peter Lake took possession of himself and, throwing his arms around what seemed like a swan, sprang to the horse's back. He was up again, exulting even as the pistol shots rang out in the cold air. Having become his accomplice in one graceful motion, the horse turned and skittered, leaning back slightly on his haunches to get breath and power for an explosive start. In that moment, Peter Lake faced his stunned pursuers and laughed at them. His entire being was one light perfect laugh. He felt the horse pitch forward, and then they raced up the street, leaving Pearly Soames and some of the Short Tail Gang backed against the iron rails, firing their pistols and cursing—all twelve of them save Pearly himself, who bit his lower lip, squinted, and began to think of new ways to trap his quarry. The noise from their many pistols was deafening.

Already out of range, Peter Lake rode at a gallop. Pounding the soft snow, passing the shuttered stores, they headed north through the awakening city in a cloud of speed.

Poncho the Pony

BY PATSY MONTANA

Get along Poncho, on your way,
We got some ground to cover today,
Ridin', rockin', ropin', rollin' pony.

Get along Poncho, travel on,
We'll hit the trail at the break of dawn,
Ridin', rockin', ropin', rollin' pony.

Get along get along,
While I yodel this song to
The rhythm of the hoofs on the ground,
For the rhythm's so strange,
It's the rhythm of the range,
Music to my ears when I hear it all around.

Get along Poncho, pony pal,
We're heading for the old corral,
Ridin', rockin', ropin', rollin' pony.

Up through the dawn
To carry on,
Riding the range together,
Poncho and I
'Neath the western sky,
And in any kind of weather.

Riding along, singing a song,
The hoofbeat rhythm beneath me,
High on the saddle,
Tie on the pack,
'Cause we ain't goin' home,
And we ain't comin' back.

Get along Poncho, on your way,
We got some ground to cover today,
Ridin', rockin', ropin', rollin' pony.

Get along Poncho, travel on,
We'll hit the trail at the break of dawn,
Ridin', rockin', ropin', rollin' pony.

Alice's Adventures in Wonderland and Through the Looking Glass

(An excerpt from "It's My Own Invention" chapter)

BY LEWIS CARROLL

WHENEVER THE HORSE STOPPED (which it did very often), he fell off in front; and whenever it went on again (which it generally did rather suddenly), he fell off behind. Otherwise, he kept on pretty well, except that he had a habit of now and then falling off sideways; and as he generally did this on the side on which Alice was walking, she soon found that it was the best plan not to walk *quite* close to the horse.

"I'm afraid you've not had much practice in riding," she ventured to say, as she was helping him up from his fifth tumble.

The Knight looked very much surprised and a little offended at the remark. "What makes you say that?" he asked, as he scrambled back into the saddle, keeping hold of Alice's hair with one hand, to save himself from falling over on the other side.

"Because people don't fall off quite so often, when they've had much practice."

"I've had plenty of practice," the Knight said very gravely: "plenty of practice!"

Alice could think of nothing better to say than "Indeed?" but she said it as heartily as she could. They went on a little way in silence after this, the Knight with his eyes shut, muttering to himself, and Alice watching anxiously for the next tumble.

"The great art of riding," the Knight suddenly began in a loud voice, waving his right arm as he spoke, "is to keep—" Here the sentence ended as suddenly as it had begun, as the Knight fell heavily on the top of his head exactly in the path where Alice was walking.

She was quite frightened this time and said in an anxious tone, as she picked him up, "I hope no bones are broken?"

"None to speak of," the Knight said, as if he didn't mind breaking two or three of them. "The great art of riding, as I was saying, is—to keep your balance properly. Like this, you know—"

He let go of the bridle and stretched out both his arms to show Alice what he meant, and this time he fell flat on his back, right under the horse's feet.

"Plenty of practice!" he went on repeating, all the time that Alice was getting him on his feet again. "Plenty of practice!"

"It's too ridiculous!" cried Alice, losing all her patience this time. "You ought to have a wooden horse on wheels, that you ought!"

"Does that kind go smoothly?" the Knight asked in a tone of great interest, clasping his arms round the horse's neck as he spoke, just in time to save himself from tumbling off again.

"Much more smoothly than a live horse," Alice said, with a little scream of laughter, in spite of all she could do to prevent it.

"I'll get one," the Knight said thoughtfully to himself. "One or two—several."

The Fly-Away Horse

BY EUGENE FIELD

Oh, a wonderful horse is the Fly-Away Horse—
Perhaps, while you slept, his shadow has swept
Through the moonlight that floats on the floor.
For it's only at night, when the stars twinkle bright,
That the Fly-Away Horse, with a neigh
And a pull at his rein and a toss of his mane,
Is up on his heels and away!
The moon in the sky,
As he gallopeth by,
Cries: "Oh! What a marvelous sight!"
And the stars in dismay
Hide their faces away
In the lap of old Grandmother Night.

It is yonder, out yonder, the Fly-Away Horse
Speedeth ever and ever away—
Over meadows and lanes, over mountains and plains,
Over streamlets that sing at their play;
And over the sea like a ghost sweepeth he,
While the ships they go sailing below,
And he speedeth so fast that the men at the mast
Adjudge him some portent of woe.
"What ho, there!" they cry,
As he flourishes by
With a whisk of his beautiful tail;

And the fish in the sea
Are as scared as can be,
From the nautilus up to the whale!

And the Fly-Away Horse seeks those faraway lands
You little folk dream of at night—
Where candy trees grow, and honey brooks flow,
And cornfields with popcorn are white;
And the beasts in the wood are ever so good
To children who visit them there—
What glory astride of a lion to ride,
Or to wrestle around with a bear!
The monkeys, they say:
"Come on, let us play,"
And they frisk in the coconut trees:
While the parrots that cling
To the peanut vines sing
Or converse with comparative ease!

Off! Scamper to bed—you shall ride him tonight!
For, as soon as you've fallen asleep,
With a jubilant neigh, he shall bear you away
Over forest and hillside and deep!
But tell us, my dear, all you see and you hear
In those beautiful lands over there,
Where the Fly-Away Horse wings his faraway course
With the wee one consigned to his care.
Then grandma will cry
In amazement: "Oh, my!"
And she'll think it could never be so.
And only we two
Shall know it is true—
You and I, little precious! Shall know!

FRANK C. PAPE

GALLOPING HORSES

Galloping Horses

After the lights of the fair are out,
When there isn't a soul about,
Away from the sides of the roundabout
gallop the galloping horses.

Tossing their tails in horsey glee,
Kicking their heels to feel they're free,
How they enjoy their nightly spree,
All those galloping horses!

In cool green grass right up to their knees,
Playing hide-and-seek amongst shrubs and trees,
You couldn't find any more gleeful "gees"
Than all those galloping horses.

For nobody comes for twopenny rides,
And nobody kicks their painted sides,
And nobody scrambles and slithers and slides
All over those galloping horses!

E.E.B

Equestrienne

BY RACHEL FIELD

Her spangles twinkle; his pale flanks shine,
Every hair of his tail is fine
And bright as a comet's; his mane blows free,
And she points a toe and bends a knee,
And while his hoofbeats fall like rain
Over and over and over again.

Runaway Pony, Runaway Dog

(An excerpt)

BY RUTH AND LATROBE CARROLL

RUNAWAY PONY, RUNAWAY DOG is the story of two best friends, a horse (Sassy) and a small bulldog (Tough Enough), who are on a long and hard journey to find their human family. Here, they have just escaped from a circus in which they were held captive.

TOUGH ENOUGH AND SASSY were moving toward the Tatum farm, too, but much more slowly and in fields far from the highway. It was good, so very good, not to be shut up inside a stockade. Every now and then the pony would prance and snort and toss his head. He would gallop for a while, his coat shining in the sun, his tail, a tawny gold, floating along the wind. Tough Enough, running in spurts to keep up with him, would leap and caper like a puppy, his wet tongue hanging out, feeling cool in the breeze of his speed.

Once, just for fun, he chased a dragonfly, its glossy wings ablaze in the sun. It zigzagged, then darted off like a bullet. His nose was savoring familiar deep-country smells: the rich earth scent, the fragrance of flowers, the pungency of weeds. But, as he and the pony crossed a highway, he sneezed as his nose sucked in the lingering sour smell of gasoline.

Whenever the pony stopped the dog would stop, too. Sometimes Tough Enough would dig in fertile soil, poking his nose deep in and sniffing earnestly before he pulled it out, plastered over at its tip with damp brown earth. Both were finding happiness in roaming through sun-warmed, sweet-scented brush, in drinking from cold, rushing brooks, in hearing the steady whisper of water over rocks, in splashing and swimming in clear ponds.

At night, it was good to feel the cool breath of the earth—good to be out when stars shone down softly through a tender haze, out among the dry rustlings of late summer and the incessant rattling and sawing of insects. Sometimes a bat would swoop close with a sweep of small dark wings and a faint fanning of air. Now and

then a distant fox would bark, sharp and clear, and always crickets chirped while fireflies sparkled against the thick darkness of pines. Rain came down. It felt cool and cleansing. On stretches bare of grass, the dust drank up the first few drops, but as they fell faster it turned to twinkling mud, soft under paws and hoofs. When the clouds parted and the sun blazed out, wet diamonds sparkled on washed leaves and bracken. Rich scents filled the air. As two noses sucked them in, Tough Enough sneezed with sheer pleasure. Sometimes fog would close in around the pair. It felt cool and damp in their noses and throats; it clung to their coats in moist beads. In the dense, drifting clouds, they found it hard to see the narrow animal trails they were following. Deep in stands of trees, squirrels scolded them. Shy, hidden birds stopped singing as they drew near, and then began again when they had passed.

It was hard for Sassy to find grass, here in the forests of the Great Smoky Mountains. Tall dense trees cut off most of the light that grass needed to grow. The pony missed the lush meadows on the Tatum farm, the oats that had helped to give him strength. He foraged mainly on leaves of young saplings and on the slender twigs of bushes.

Both animals were lean. Their ribs showed plainly, and Sassy's hip bones stuck out. Their coats had lost all luster and had a ragged look. Tough Enough no longer moved lightly, for the pads of his paws were sore. Little burrs and thorns sometimes stuck between his toes; he would stop and gnaw at them. Hunger was gradually cutting down his strength. But through the dragging minutes, he and the pony kept plodding on, and the minutes turned into hours and the hours into days.

They had climbed to lofty ground close to the park's southeast boundary when they heard distant hounds giving tongue, from far below. The hounds were in full cry, as if they had struck a fresh trail and had started to follow it. Sassy and Tough Enough had often heard just such distant sounds in the mountains back of the Tatum farm. They did not stop their onward push.

Little by little the deep singing changed. It was splitting up—coming in sharp, short, eager bursts. Plainly, the trail was growing hot, the pack was nearing its quarry. As that grim chorus came ever louder and fiercer, the dog and the pony grew apprehensive. Tough Enough gave an asking growl. Sassy halted. He looked down at the dog, his eyes large with alarm, then he swung his head high, nostrils flaring, ears thrust forward. He lifted a foot and stamped it down. A harsh sound, shrill with warning, forced itself out of his throat.

All of a sudden, five half-starved hounds came crackling out of dry brush. They were panting, their sides heaving, for they had been racing uphill. Ugly-looking mongrels—the biggest a Plott hound—they seemed little else but skin and bones and sinews. They bared savage teeth.

They fixed their eyes—staring, red-rimmed—on Tough Enough and Sassy. Their owners, poor mountain farmers, had not given them enough to eat. So the gaunt creatures had banded together. They were experienced marauders: killers of chickens, calves, sheep, and other dogs.

The shock of danger poured new strength into Tough Enough. His dragging weakness ended on a surge of excited blood. Forgotten was the pain of sore paws. His ears went back, the skin above his spine tingled, every hair erect. He snarled fiercely. The pony was showing his teeth and the gleaming whites of his eyes. He knew he must fight for his life and for Tough Enough. His dull fatigue was gone; his old energy and speed came back. He did not wait to be attacked. With a shrill trumpeting he charged. In mid course he swerved sharply and lashed out with his hoofs.

One of the hounds, struck squarely in the ribs, went flying as if hit by a mighty hammer. Swinging part way around, the pony reared, forefeet poised, then brought his hoofs down on a mongrel who had turned tail, surprised by the onslaught. The blow sent him sprawling. He struggled to his feet and dragged himself away.

For a moment, the three hounds who were left were full of startled confusion. They had never before picked a victim of this sort, a pony with the blood of wild horses in his veins.

Recovering their courage, they began to circle Sassy, keeping at a cautious distance, but now and then making short, threatening rushes. Again and again he charged them, but they were as cunning as wolves, skilled at swerving and dodging and leaping out of reach.

The pony's coat was dark with sweat, whitely flecked with lather. Fatigue had begun to drag at him again, but he was fighting it. The big Plott hound—he seemed to be the leader—was the slyest and most persistently aggressive.

After each retreat, he had darted forward so smoothly that his body seemed to flow. Now he was ready, watching, waiting. He saw his chance. He sprang at one of Sassy's legs, to slash the large tendon there. The hounds had paid little heed to Tough Enough; Sassy had been the menace. But Tough Enough had not stood still.

He was much quicker and nimbler than any of the hounds many times his size. A bundle of taut nerves and wiry muscles, he had been here, there, and everywhere, dodging Sassy's hoofs, snarling at Sassy's attackers, now and then getting in a nip and darting away. Now, as the Plott hound leaped at Sassy, Tough Enough jumped, too, at twice the speed. Before the hound's teeth could close on the pony's leg, Tough Enough seized one of his long, limp ears. His jaws closed and gripped and held. The hound's head swiveled convulsively. He missed his aim. Yelping, he whirled round and round, trying to shake the dog off. Tough Enough, sailing in circles, hung on.

Sassy turned to look. Instantly, the other two hounds rushed at him. He swung around to defend himself. He drove them many yards away, but not before one of them had made a long gash in his left shoulder.

The Plott hound, still trying to rid himself of Tough Enough, went wheeling close to a tree. The little dog felt a stunning blow, a flash of intense pain as he was slammed against the trunk. His grip loosened. He dropped to the ground. The big hound stood for an uncertain moment, panting and dizzy. Then his jaws, eager to seize and crush, groped downward. They opened, reaching for Tough Enough's backbone.

Before they could close, Sassy's hoofs flashed into action. They shot out. They caught the Plott hound in the flank and sent him, howling, off into the bushes. With their leader out of the fight, the two remaining mongrels had had enough. They went slinking off. Silently, with heads and tails low, they padded away into green dimness.

Even after they had disappeared, the dog and the pony stayed alert, suspicious. Both were trembling. Would the hounds come back, perhaps from a different direction? Minutes passed, long and watchful and waiting. Now and then, Tough Enough would lick at a sluggish trickle of blood meandering down Sassy's left foreleg. Little by little the flow lessened.

The woods: the aromatic smell of sun-warmed resin oozing from pines; the honey fragrance of sourwood blossoms; the call of a flicker, a single note repeated very fast: wet-wet-wet-wet-wet-wet-wet—but no scents or noises that might mean new danger.

Tough Enough relaxed. His legs let his body down until he was lying on the trampled ground in a weary half-daze. The pony's muzzle dipped lower and lower.

After a rest, Sassy lifted his head. He shook himself. As if that were a signal, Tough Enough stood up slowly. The fight had left him stiff and aching. A faint protest, part growl and part whine, came squeezing out of his throat. Gently, he and Sassy touched noses. Once more, they began to push themselves along. As they plodded onward at a slackening pace, their stiffness eased a little; but their weariness increased. Tough Enough's tail was drooping. Loss of blood had weakened Sassy still more. His feet dragged and, twice, he stumbled. Both animals had to take frequent rests. When the round blaze of the morning sun was burning well up in the sky, they reached a hot dusty lane. They followed it to a wider dirt road, slowly moving down into a valley. Some deep awareness told them it was taking them toward home. But their strength was almost gone.

Suddenly, Tough Enough whimpered; his nose had picked up an absorbing scent. It seemed familiar. . . . Could it be . . . ? A tingle of excitement raced along his spine. That scent—it was growing stronger—yes, that scent was Beanie's!

A warm feeling flowed all through him; he began to give eager cries. Hope brought him new strength. It went down into his legs; they sent him forward briskly; it spread all along his tail and made it whip back and forth. Following Beanie's trail, he picked up other nearby scents: Ma Tatum's, then Pa's—and next, mixed together and crisscrossing, Buck's trail and Irby's and Serena's and Annie Mae's. And, all the while, his excitement was yipping out of his throat.

The pony gave a questioning whinny. He was forcing himself to follow the dog but lagging heavily behind; often Tough Enough had to stop and wait, yapping at Sassy to urge him on.

At last they drew near a little white church. Tough Enough led Sassy to the door. His newfound energy was leaving him. He crawled up three steps, each an aching effort. The pony was close behind him, unsteady at the knees. They went through the door, open to let in fresh air, and began to walk uncertainly along the middle aisle. Church members were standing up, loudly singing a hymn. In front, the minister, erect and facing them, was joining in.

He was the first to see the dog and the pony. He stopped singing abruptly. Other people, too, caught sight of the animals. A startled man in a back pew, then another and still another, moved out into the aisle to catch them.

But before the men could stop them, Tough Enough had found the Tatums. He uttered a high, hoarse, squeezed-out bark, almost like a scream. He did his best to jump up on Beanie, but his legs gave way beneath him. He dropped down at Beanie's feet and lay there with his nose touching one of Beanie's shoes. The pony went dragging close to Beanie. He was almost too weak to stand, but he pushed his soft muzzle against the boy's neck. He nickered gently. Beanie hugged him. Then he picked Tough Enough up in his arms and pressed his cheek against the little dog's head. Mixed feelings were swirling in him. He was almost bursting with joy—but full of sorrow, too, to see how thin and weak both animals were. Pa Tatum led Sassy out of the church and to the old truck. Beanie and the other Tatums followed.

Men helped Pa lift the pony up into the truck; he didn't weigh much now. They laid him on the floor. Beanie and the other young Tatums climbed up into the back. Serena sat down close to Sassy. She lifted his head into her lap and cradled it there and stroked it.

"We'll be leavin' directly," Pa told the men who had helped. "We'll take these poor critters home and nurse 'em and feed 'em till they feel frisky again, full of get up and git."

Safe in Beanie's arms, Tough Enough closed his eyes. Slowly, he opened one of them. It was a happy eye. Now, at last, he and the pony were back with the people they loved. They were going home.

Cowboy Poem

I started up the trail
about June twenty-third;
Been punching Texas cattle
for the C and S herd.
Singin' ti yi yippe,
yippe aye, yippe aye,
ti yi yippe,
yippe aye. . . .

A True Horse Tale

A CAPTAIN OF CAVALRY in a French regiment mentions that a horse belonging to his company, being, due to age, unable to eat his hay or grind his oats, was fed for two months by two horses on his right and left, who ate with him. These two horses, drawing the hay out of the rack, chewed it, and then put it before the old horse, and did the same with the oats, which he was then able to eat.

Acknowledgments

WE WISH TO THANK the following properties, whose cooperation has made this unique collection possible. All care has been taken to trace ownership of these selections and to make a full acknowledgment. If any errors or omissions have occurred, they will be corrected in subsequent editions, provided notification is sent to the compiler.

Front Cover	Emma L. Brock, from *The Plug-Horse Derby,* 1955.
Front Flap	Anonymous, n.d., from *Rusty Pete of the Lazy AB*, 1930.
Endpapers	Anonymous, n.d.
Half-Title Page	Willy Pogany, from *Gulliver's Travels*, 1924.
Frontispiece	Jacques Brown, from *Country Joys,* 1928.
Title Page	Emma L. Brock, from *The Plug-Horse Derby,* 1955.
Copyright Page	John Reynolds, from *Horse Nonsense*, 1933.
Dedication	Robert Frankenberg, from *Black Beauty,* 1960.
Contents	James Schucker, from *Big Black Horse*, 1953.
12	B. Butler, from *Animals Stories and Pictures*, circa 1920.
13	H. Goodwine, circa 1890.
14–17	Zhenya Gay, from *Wonderful Things!* 1954.
18	Anonymous, rodeo poster, circa 1930.
19	Ernest Nordli, from *Roy Rogers on the Double R Ranch*, 1951.
20	Anonymous, rodeo poster, circa 1910.
22–31	Wesley Dennis, from *Lance and His First Horse*, 1949..
32–34	Philip Pimlott, from *Blackie's Children's Annual*, 1932.
35	C. W. Anderson, from *Black, Bay, and Chestnut*, 1939.
37–44	Emma L. Brock, from *The Plug-Horse Derby*, 1955.
48	Florence Mary Anderson, circa 1920.

49	Anonymous, n.d.
50	Margaret Evans Price, from *Myths and Enchantment Tales*, 1924.
51	B. Artzvbasheff, circa 1910.
52–61	Wesley Dennis, from *Five O'Clock Charlie*, 1962.
62	Anonymous, n.d.
64	Nils Kreuger, 1902.
65–73	Dorothy Henderson Pinch, from *Happy Horsemanship*, 1962.
74	Theodore Gericault, *Head of a White Horse*, circa 1815.
76	C. W. Anderson, from *Black, Bay, and Chestnut*, 1939.
77	Anonymous, n.d.

78	Anonymous, magazine illustration, circa 1930.
79	Anonymous, from *The Picture Book of Domestic Animals*, 1891.
80	Anonymous, circa 1920.
83–88	Doris Fogler, from *Rusty Pete of the Lazy AB*, 1930.
91	Harper Johnson, from *Lone Hunter's Gray Pony,* 1954.
92	Anonymous, magazine illustration, circa 1950.
94–104	James Schucker, from *Big Black Horse*, 1953.
106	Holling C. and Lucille Holling, from *The Book of Cowboys*, 1934.
107	Doris Fogler, from *Rusty Pete of the Lazy AB*, 1930.
108	Holling C. and Lucille Holling, from *The Book of Cowboys*, 1934.
109	Doris Fogler, from *Rusty Pete of the Lazy AB*, 1930.
110–117	Neda Dokic, from *Winter's Tale*, 2009.
118	Kerbit, calendar illustration, circa 1940.
119	Anonymous, n.d.
120	Leonard Weisgard, from *Alice's Adventures in Wonderland,* 1949.
122–123	A. H. Watson, from *Alice's Adventures in Wonderland*, 1939.
124	Gustave Tenggren, 1927.
125	Anonymous, n.d.
127	Frank C. Pape, from *The Russian Story Book*, 1916.
128	Anonymous, n.d.
129	Honor Appleton, 1930.
130–139	Ruth and Latrobe Carroll, from *Runaway Pony*, 1963.
140	Jack Merryweather, from *Cowboy Sam and the Rustlers*, 1952.
141	Anonymous, circa 1870.
143	R. Farrington Elwell, magazine illustration, circa 1910.
145	Anonymous, postcard, circa 1900.
Endpapers	Anonymous, n.d.
Back Cover	Honor Appleton, 1930.